Snag and Me
Flying in a Jenny

By
Joseph A. Johnston

Copyright © 2005 Joseph A. Jonhston

First Published 2005
Penman Publishing, Inc.

All rights reserved. Use of any part of this
publication without prior written consent of the
author is an infringement of the copyright law.

Joseph A. Johnston

Snag & Me
Flying in a Jenny

Manufactured in the United States of America.

Cover and inside illustrations by the author.

In Memory of Chris Becker
February 28, 2005

Goodbye Little Trooper

Yes my Little Trooper, you fought a good fight every step of the way,
But sadly now it's time to rest and let God have His way.
Never have we seen one so determined and full of "Yes I Can,"
You have proven to me and others that you were quite a little man.

The endless suffering, you can now leave it all behind and hurt no more,
As Angels lift you up and carry you to that eternal Golden Shore.
Our hearts are aching and the tears fall like a summer rain,
But God knows best, for He didn't want to see you live in such pain.

Yes, Heaven has a new Angel, Chris Becker is his precious name,
Now he can run and laugh, chasing moonbeams is his new game.
He can see his old friends who wait anxiously at Heaven's door,
The ones who fought the same battles and have gone on before.

We will all miss you Chris, and the memories of your long and gallant fight,
The many lessons you taught us, standing tall, marching toward God's light.
Perhaps you knew more than we about the final outcome on that fateful day,
But you didn't want to sadden us and tell us you had to go away.

Now your Mom and Dad, awesome heroes too in everyone's eye,
They set aside life, standing vigilant by your side urging you for one more try.
But all the medicines, all the doctors, all the prayers seemed for naught,
For this was a battle for everyone who loved you, yes we all fought.

So now we bid you farewell, my Little Trooper, farewell 'til then,
When some bright morning God will let us see your happy face again.
Rest easy, enjoy your Heavenly home, now you can try out your new wings,
As you look back with that smile from the land where the Angels sing.

God Bless,
Grandpa Joe & Grandma Margie
And Snag and Me

A Note From the Author

Dear Readers…again I sit and try to think of something spiffy to say as a way of introducing my latest little story of *Snag and Me*. This story was originally written in 1994. I don't know why I pursued this one at this time, but a set of unique circumstances came into my life which caused me to take a second look. In February this past year, I had lost a dear little fan by the name of Chris Becker of Tampa, FL. This wasn't easy, for I had followed his ordeal for five years. When the sad news arrived, I was broken hearted, to say the least. Though we never met, I felt I knew him pretty well because of the daily e-mails his mom and dad wrote telling of his struggle to survive. So, while sitting around moping and sad as one can be when receiving such news, I was also thinking of some way to keep Chris's memory alive for years to come. Then I looked at this story again and thought, "You know, I bet I could fit Chris in here somehow and make him a star with the boys."... meaning Snag and Earl D., of course.

I wasn't sure how receptive his folks would be to this idea, so I sent an e-mail asking permission to use his name and some of his persona in this story. They readilly agreed. I also sent them a draft of the story when I got it mostly completed to see if it was okay with them. Again, they agreed. His mom was gracious enough to write some details about Chris which appears at the end of the story. So please read those too. I think it will warm your heart a bit and also help you realize that parents have an awesome level of determination when it comes to trying to keep their children around. I am humbled by it all. I hope you like my attempts and that you can grasp just a little of the Little Trooper as I mix him into the story. He was one bright little fellow, smart beyond his years. We will all miss him.

v

Thank you again for your continuing support. Without nice folks like you picking up my stories and reading about two little guys growing up in the country, life would be pretty boring for this old retired grandpa. I also want especially to thank my wonderful and supportive family, my friends, and my super great publisher, for allowing and helping me make this dream come true.

God Bless and happy reading…

Joe Johnston
Fayetteville, TN

CHARACTERS AND ROLES

Earl D. McHenry—The main character and narrator of the story. Cautious, but tolerant of his best pal, Snag.

Wilfred (Snag) Galloway—The second main character and Earl D.'s best friend. Always one step away from mischief.

Jeb McHenry—Earl D.'s stern, hard-working and loving father.

Pearl McHenry—Earl D.'s mother and the world's best cook.

Nell Faye McHenry—Earl D.'s *uppity* elder sister, who thinks she knows it all.

Percy McHenry—Earl D.'s baby brother, noted for his bad table manners and lots of grunting.

Laroy Galloway—Snag's hard-working father and best friend of the McHenrys.

Lois Patricia Galloway—Snag's mother, always ready to pull her hair out over Snag's shenanigans.

Chris—A new little friend the boys meet at the park. A bright and friendly fellow, Chris is a friend of everyone would enjoy having.

Gus 'Sparks' Einberger—Grumpy old mechanic for the flying circus; also grandfather of Chris.

Capt. 'Crazy' Ray B. Ricker—Supposedly the world's most famous aviator and a great storyteller.

The Sweeny Family—Entire Gospel choir at Corner Baptist Church.

Bubba Jean Fritzwater—Renowned female schoolyard bully, seemingly intent on making Snag and Earl D. miserable.

"Skip"—Snag's faithful canine companion, a mongrel akin to all other dogs around.

vii

A SCARY AND STORMY NIGHT

There I was in a deep dream world, dreaming that Snag and me were out beating on an old hollow log way down in some deep, dark woods. We were laughing like crazy and having lots of fun beating on this old hollow log with some big sticks. The sound seemed unreal and extra loud. The beating sounds would make so much racket and each time we hit the log it would cause this mysterious bright flash of light. All the noise and flashing caused a passel of raccoons to run out one end of the log. With each loud whack of the stick, there came another bright flash and another batch of raccoons would run out of the log, one after the other. I was telling myself in the dream that this just didn't seem right... and it wasn't.

What was really happening at that moment wasn't a dream at all. It was more like a nightmare! I mean a real live nightmare! I was jarred plumb awake by this loud booming noise that caused me to sit straight up in bed as my dream faded real fast. I'm sure the hairs on my head were standing straight up from pure fear. The whole house was shaking, windows rattling with lots of lightening flashes going on all around us. I knew in that instant of waking up that something was dreadfully wrong.

I jumped out of bed as Little Percy, my baby brother, started screaming and grabbing me around my arms. He didn't know what was going on and neither did I, except I knew we were having a real bad storm, the likes of which I had never seen.

Mama came rushing around shutting the windows and then to our bedside. Grabbing us both up, she quickly led us into the kitchen. There was Papa sitting with his Bible open trying to read something in the flickering light of our kerosene lamp. Mama had her housecoat pulled up around her tightly. Papa had on his overalls instead of his nightshirt. Nell Faye had her coat on too. It looked like everybody was getting ready to go someplace... all except Little Percy and me. Mercy, where would we be going on a night like this?

I just knew in my country boy mind that something was bad wrong for Papa, Mama and Nell Faye to be up at this hour nearly dressed and all. I was convinced from all the serious looks on everyone's face that I wasn't the only one scared senseless. For certain, this wasn't no ordinary-everyday thunderstorm like I had seen before in my young life. I knew it had been extra hot today and poor Mama and the rest of us had been snapping and canning beans for the past three days. Even while we were sitting on the back porch snapping the beans, Mama and the rest of us were wishing for a cool breeze or a little shower to cool things off. Guess we got more than we wished for.

I was trying to think clearly, which was a tough job even when things were normal, but it was even harder to do with my teeth chattering like crazy and holding on to my knees to slow them down from shaking so badly. With all the thundering and lightening going on, how could anyone think of doing anything except being scared out of your wits? Even Nell Faye, my older and normally unafraid sister, was shaking with tears in her eyes. This wasn't a good sign either.

This had to be one fierce storm to be sure to cause all this fear around me. KA-BOOOOMMMMMM... as more loud claps of thunder kept booming one after another along with several bright blue flashes of lighting. The sky outside the kitchen windows was filled with endless bright flashes. The rain was beating fiercely against the side of the house and our tin roof. I knew Papa had prayed for a little rain of late too because things were getting more than a little dry around here. I think, like us, he may have asked for too much.

Some of the thunderclaps were so powerful they just shook the whole house over and over again, causing our pots, pans, and the dishes to rattle like they had a mind of their own. Mama was afraid the dishes would all tumble off the cabinet shelves as she and Nell Faye rushed to lay them flat. They were moving the jars of beans around too to keep them from falling off the shelves.

Maybe the Good Lord was mad at the whole world when He sends a storm like this. I wasn't sure what we had done to upset Him so but I was hoping Papa would get the right words going to let the Good Lord know that we are with Him always and hope He's with us always—especially right now!

Little Percy was really whimpering as Mama held him close trying to calm him down. Mercy, I could stand a little of that hugging about now too, but she had enough to worry about, so I just sat there and shook. Nell Faye was doing a pretty good job of shaking too. I think the only one that wasn't shaking was Papa.

Now the winds were picking up good and roaring really loud as they whipped around the house, causing the windows to rattle like they were going to fall plumb out. We were all bug-eyed and looking around at everything as all the pots and pans were rattling like they were going to fall off the wall hangers. We were wondering what was going to break loose next. That's about the time when Papa told us that we might be getting a "TORNADO."

TALES OF TORNADOES AS THINGS GO FROM BAD TO WORSE

I had never seen one but to hear other folks talk, these are storms that you don't want to come around for a visit. To country folks, the dread of a tornado is something that was feared all the time during the springtime and early summer. But here we were already into July and I guess we weren't supposed to be getting storms like this. I guess we didn't ask the Good Lord about it either.

We would often hear a lot of about tornadoes at times tearing up land and farms someplace else, but never this close to our little farm.

Papa had us all hold hands as he prayed aloud. "Lord I know we aren't without sin, but Lord if you could please spare this poor family, we'll continue to serve you as best we can… just like we've always tried to do. Lord we ask that you favor us with mercy and Lord we ask you spare not just us, but our neighbors too."

I didn't hear his AMEN but I did hear this new racket going on right over our heads! It sounded like rocks hitting our tin roof. We sat there, all scared out of our minds. I yelled out: "Papa is that the hail and brimstone the Preacher talks about all the time?"

Papa looked at me with concern but eased my mind a little as he said it was just the hail and no brimstone. Well, I guess that was a little good news if any was to be had at the moment, but what he said next only caused our fears to rise a little higher.

"Now what we're hearing hitting the roof is hail. From the racket it's making I'd say it's pretty good size. This could mean that it's possible for a tornado to be right close or it will be soon."

We didn't have a fraidy hole like some folks had which meant we didn't have no place to run and hide. So Papa did the only thing we could do at the moment. "All right, we need to try and protect ourselves best we can with some kind of strong cover in case the roof blows off. Let's all get under this heavy old oak table my grandpa McHenry built way back yonder."

Without waiting for a nudge, we all quickly scampered under the kitchen table, then turned the benches over to sort of block us in. Papa rushed into the other room and quickly returned with some quilts that he threw over us to offer, I supposed, a little more protection. Papa managed to wiggle under there with us. Now we were cramped in there real tight, all huddled in a mess of arms and legs and hanging on to one another. Whew, it was getting hot as an oven too.

Mama was worried as she asked Papa a question out of fear. "Jeb, if the house blows away where in goodness would we all sleep?"

I guess Papa was just hoping and praying like the rest of us that this tornado storm wouldn't kill us all as he tried to answer Mama. "Pearl, if it blows away, and we don't get blowed away with it, we'll sleep in the barn if it's still here, or somebody's barn until we build another one. But I don't think it'll go anywhere. Grandpa McHenry built this place with heavy timber, so I think all we have to do is hang on and pray."

I was hoping he was right about the house. I knew this old oak table was very heavy from trying to lift one end of it once or twice. I was sure Great-grandpa McHenry, way back when he built this house many years ago, meant for the table to last along with the house. The table was so heavy that I couldn't recall it ever being moved too often for anything, even cleaning the floor. Maybe it was safer under here than anyplace else in the house.

About that time we heard this new sound as the winds was blowing louder and louder sounding sort of like a freight train roaring down on us. Along with all that new sound, the unending lightening and thunder crashes with that hard driving rain continued.

Little Percy was sobbing pretty loud himself as Mama was hanging on to him tightly. As a matter of fact we were just scared flat to death that we might get blown away. There wasn't anything else we could do but huddle under that old table and wait for whatever was going to happen. There we were just all tangled up together hanging on to each other for dear life. If the worse came to past and we all got blown away, at least we'd all be together.

THE STORM LETS UP

After what seemed like forever, the hail noise stopped, but the rain kept on. The lightening seemed

SNAG & ME – A FLYING IN A JENNY 7

to be less now and the winds were dying down. We started breathing a sigh of relief as we slowly crawled out from under the table. Mama and Nell Faye folded the quilts back up and returned them to the bedrooms. I know it felt good to get out of that oven we were in. Whew, we were cooking.

Papa glanced out the windows and then reached up on the wall and grabbed the old lantern off a hook. With a strike of a match he had it lit. As he began to open the door to the back porch, Mama came rushing back into the kitchen and commenced yelling at him. "Jeb, where in heavens name are you going?"

Papa turned and told us to sit tight. "Now y'all stay here. I've got to go check on the livestock and see if we still have a barn, or any animals left." This only caused Mama to get even more excited. "Jeb, why don't you at least wait until it stops raining so hard?"

I guess Mama's word was enough to make him wait. Papa was fidgety and nothing soothed him at this point, so he went on out to the porch anyway as we followed right in behind him. There was lots of distant lightening off toward the mountains. The cool breeze that was still gusting only caused us to shake like leaves on a tree. We noticed the rocking chair was knocked over and the wash tubs were missing from the porch, along with the wash basin, towels and such that normally hung near the well. No telling where they were.

Mama told Papa we had to have them tubs and washbasin or else we'd be wearing dirty clothes along with a dirty face until we got some new ones. Papa assured her that tubs and basin would be found first thing in the morning.

THE STORM LEAVES A MESS

I rushed back inside and quickly put on my overalls 'cause I wanted to go with Papa and see what was all tore up too. I was praying that everything would be okay. I didn't want to lose ole Charlie, our faithful family mule, or our cows, Lulu Belle and Miss Nellie, our two shy cats Mr. Smoky and Miss Midnight. I would miss the chickens and even the pigs. Mercy, we needed them all.

From listening to Papa and Mama tell their stories about these kinds of storms, sometimes a body would wake up in another county with no house, no relatives, no nothing, and mostly near dead.

I was thinking that would be just too terrible to live after that. 'Course, my wild imagination was worse than the real thing and caused me to shiver all over. I knew I had to get my mind off that as I rushed back out onto the porch.

I pulled on Mama's arm as she turned to look at me. "Mama, you reckon Snag and his family came through this storm okay?"

Mama tried to calm my fears about my best pal in the whole world and his folks as she replied, "Well, Earl D., I'm praying if the Good Lord let us live through all this, that He let them live too. Now we have to pray that everyone around here was spared."

I had a sound of woe in my voice standing there holding her hand tightly… "I sure hope you're right Mama. I don't know what I'd do if my best chum got blowed away."

We all watched Papa as he was swinging the lantern one way and then another but even with the lantern we couldn't tell what was blown away or not. The water racing down through the yard looked like a muddy river flowing. We saw lots of limbs and such so we knew we had some mighty powerful winds.

GOING WITH PAPA TO CHECK FOR STORM DAMAGE

At long last when the rain slowed to a drizzle, Papa and me eased off the back porch. We had to watch where we stepped because of all the tree limbs lying all over the place as we picked our way through all this and the mud down to the barn. I just about turned and ran back to the porch when Papa announced that at times, water moccasins would be washed up in storms like this. But he felt since we were pretty far from the creek that we didn't have anything to fear. I hope he was right… and here I was barefooted to boot!

As we walked, Papa steered us over to the edge of the garden. Again he began swinging the lantern to and fro trying to see what damage there was. He was worried that our crops might have some heavy damage from all the wind and hail as he voiced his concern to me.

"Earl D., I'm glad we got a lot of the beans, tomatoes and some corn picked. If we had of waited another day to get them down to the livery stable to sell, we'd be in a heap of a mess. Now if the Good Lord didn't spare the crops that were left, this could cause us a few problems. If it's bad, there ain't enough time left in this season to start over. We didn't hold back any tomatoes or corn for canning, you know."

Now I had a new worry on my mind, wondering how in the world we'd eat if we didn't have a garden left. I knew a body could only drink so much buttermilk until they blew up. I loved buttermilk but even too much of a good thing isn't good for you, according to Mama.

10 JOSEPH A. JOHNSTON

I just didn't want to get too full of buttermilk. At least we still had lots of things canned under the house in our dug out root cellar and the fresh jars of beans in the kitchen. At least we would last for a while, but then what would we eat?

"Papa, we'll starve to death," I shouted in a scared tone of voice. Papa, sensing my fear, tried to calm me down with some good words I had heard him call Mama, and even recall Snag saying the same thing; words that I would always remember when trouble is about.

"Earl D., if the Good Lord leads you into a mess in life, He will lead you out of it just as well. You just have to keep your faith, son. Now is not the time to be fretting or adding worry to your young mind. For sure we won't starve. We may run short on a few things, but we'll make it with God's help just like other bad times."

I was hoping he was right, but I didn't remember any bad times before. Maybe that was before I was born, or when I was a young'un still crawling around. I guess Papa's earlier prayer to spare us was answered, but he forgot to ask the Good Lord to spare our garden too. 'Course we couldn't see anything out toward the garden. That would have to wait until morning's first light. I was just hoping Papa was right.

STORM DAMAGE RIGHT IN FRONT OF US

When we got to the barn, we noticed one of the large doors was completely blown off the barn and lying to one side. At least it was still around and mostly in one piece. We walked inside with Papa holding the lantern high so we could see the stalls where Charlie, our one and only faithful family mule, was stirring. He seemed to be grinning and acted like he was glad to see

SNAG & ME – A FLYING IN A JENNY   11

us. I guess this storm spooked him pretty good too. Our cows seemed a little skittish but calmed down as Papa rubbed their necks and talked to them. Charlie, seeing all this, let loose a little mule talk as he sort of whinnied a little. Papa laughed out a little. "Suppose Charlie's glad that storm is over too, Earl D." I laughed with him as I replied, "Him and me too, Papa." Our two cats were up in the loft meowing away like they were happy this storm was over too.

We couldn't tell if any of the roofs had blown off the barn or the house. That would have to wait until morning too.

After checking on the pigs and looking at the chicken coop, we were glad everything was still around. Papa, thinking we had done all we could for the moment, turned and told me that was all for tonight. We walked back toward the porch through all the limbs and mud again. My feet were like two heavy stones from all the mud I had caked on them. I knew a lot of scuffing in the grass was in order...if I could find a patch or two. As we passed by the smokehouse I saw our two washtubs. I was glad we found them 'cause I didn't want to have to wear dirty clothes.

Papa led us back with the tubs. This pleased Mama but she also added, "Well, looks like work is still in store for me and you all won't have to go dirty after all."

With the light of lantern we spotted the washbasin just at the edge of the porch. Now we would have clean clothes and no dirty hands and faces.

We hung the tubs back up on the hooks on the porch wall. Then we all walked back inside to the kitchen table. Mama was asking a thousand questions as Papa raised his hands for quiet. When it got quiet again, he had us all join hands as he thanked the Good Lord for sparing us. After the Amen, he told Mama and the rest that everything seemed to be okay except for the barn door. "Now we couldn't see much of the garden, so that'll have to wait till morning to see how bad off we really are."

GETTING OVER THE STORM SHAKES WITH BUTTERMILK

The clock said it was nearly three in the morning. I was so nervous, I wasn't sure I could even go back to sleep. Mama had us all drink a glass of buttermilk to calm us down. I wasn't sure if that would work or not.

After washing my feet off, and getting Mama's approval, I headed for the bed. Putting my nightshirt back on, I laid back down, listening to the calm breathing of Little Percy who was already in dreamland, no longer scared out of his wits. How I wished I could fall asleep so easy. I guess little boys like Percy didn't fret or worry so much about things once it was over. I wasn't sure why I worried so much about things... especially things I couldn't do a flit about anyway.

I did notice one thing; it was getting awfully stuffy. With a little begging, Mama finally gave me permission to raise the window again. A nice, cool welcomed breeze came rushing in. Now I could sleep.

I shut my eyes saying another prayer of thanks but still fearing what we would find in the morning. I said a prayer for my pal Snag and his family too, and all the other folks... even Bubba Jean Fritzwater. Then I must have drifted off to sleep. The next thing I knew was more PAIN!

THE PAIN OF PUTTING UP WITH A BOSSY SISTER

My waking up was sudden and painful. That stinking Nell Faye was trying to twist my big toe off

SNAG & ME – A FLYING IN A JENNY   13

again! I was hollering loud enough to wake the dead. She finally turned it loose, looking at me with that grin of hers. "Earl D., Mama said for you to get up NOW!" With that she turned and pranced back into the kitchen to help Mama with breakfast.

I had tears in my eyes from the paining. Why did she do this to me and how come Mama let her do it all the time? I was making myself a promise that one of these days I was gonna get up early and go wring her toe till she hollered. I wanted to see her tear up too just to get a feeling of what she had put me through so many times. It's a wonder I have a big toe left and they don't grow crooked from all that wringing she's done ever so long.

At breakfast Papa, who had already been up and about, told us that it appeared the roof over the house was in pretty good shape, but the barn suffered a few pieces of tin pulled up. Then I was told I would have to go to the store after a bit and get some nails and such so Papa could fix everything.

Now this bit of news pleased me a whole bunch. As I was getting all happy about going to the store, Mama put a damper of sorts on my happiness for the moment.

"Jeb, I need Earl D. to clean up some of the back yard before he goes traipsing off to the store." Papa just nodded his head and took off back out the door toward the barn.

I ate breakfast slow 'cause I knew a lot of work awaited me in the back yard. Then I'd be busy the rest of the day helping Papa. I knew this meant that I might not be able to go fishing with Snag later on today, as we have been doing about three times a week since school was out.

As we all expected, the yard was full of limbs and leaves. This meant a big clean up job for sure. Papa

14 JOSEPH A. JOHNSTON

was taking a dipper of water and talking to me at the same time. "Now, Earl D., son, I need you to get a rush on the yard cleaning 'cause I'll need your help to raise the barn door back up." I nodded my head... "Yessir Papa, I'll hurry as fast as I can."

I picked up several armloads of limbs and piled them so we could burn them later or use some for wood around the boiling pot on washday. Then I headed for the barn to help Papa with the door. It was heavy but with both of us huffing and puffing we managed to get it upright and leaning against the barn. Papa said we would hang it after I got back with the screws. That sounded good to me. I was plumb out of steam from just that little lifting job. Whew... no rest for the weary.

THE GARDEN CORN IS A-SAGGING...NELL FAYE'S TONGUE GOES A-WAGGING

I walked with Papa as we looked over the garden. Lots of plants were blown down but the rows of string beans seemed to have come through the storm okay. The tomato plants seemed to be pretty much okay too. Even the corn seemed to have weathered it fairly good with only a few stalks really broken over. We walked out and pulled some of the stalks back up, hoping the roots didn't get busted off. That would be a blessing for sure. Papa looked up at the sky and uttered, "Lord you've blessed us richly. Thank you!"

I must have been standing still too long 'cause I heard Mama yelling something from the back porch, so Papa sent me scurrying to see what she wanted.

She was pointing at the yard. I knew this meant for me to finish cleaning it up. I was wishing for some help from Nell Faye but she had already sat down at the churn working away and reading a book at the

SNAG & ME – A FLYING IN A JENNY   15

same time. I knew she could have done that later. I guess I was lucky; I got the chore of cleaning up all the limbs and then trying to sweep the yard all by myself. The ground was still too wet to make the broom work right. All this sweating just got my dander up. It was upsetting to work and work and it still didn't look right. Nothing was going right for me it seemed.

One other endless pain was sitting on the porch hollering at me. Nell Faye wouldn't let me move two feet without yelling out that I had missed something.

Mama came out on the porch to try and tell her to stop pestering me.

I was happy that Mama said what she said 'cause my constant yelling at her to shut her big mouth just didn't do any good. Mercy, I was in need of some relief for this poor country boy... but I knew it wouldn't last and it didn't. Nell Faye didn't waste a minute until she blurted out: "Mama he's missed so many things. If I don't tell him what's he's missing, we'll still have a messy yard. And, can you imagine what the Preacher would think if he happens to ride up to see how we are? That'd be the world's worst embarrassment ever! Why I could never show my face at church again."

Mama must have thought some of her bellyaching was just pure horse fodder and mostly funny as she started laughing. "Nell Faye, I don't think the preacher would be looking at our yard or anyone's yard after last night. He'd only be concerned that we are still here and breathing. So would you do me a favor? How about sparing your brother and me all that yelling. You two are giving me a headache and it's not even dinner time yet." With that, Mama turned and headed back to the kitchen.

Nell Faye gave me one of her famous looks of evil. I just smiled and stuck my tongue out at her. She blurted

16   JOSEPH A. JOHNSTON

out, "It's not fair you get to go to the store all the time, numbskull. I think we oughta draw straws to see who's going. You game, pea-brain?"

Now if I was to call her names like that, she'd bellyache so much to Mama I'd find myself in a jam. I knew she had me between a rock and a hard place. She knew I don't take a dare for anything. If I say no, she'll call me sissy, scardy cat and everything else. I just ignored her and kept to my cleaning up the yard.

MAMA CHECKS THE YARD FOR FLAWS AND NELL FAYE WANTS TO DRAW STRAWS

Sometimes little miracles happen. I had been witness to few just recently. The storm didn't blow us away; our garden wasn't torn up; and Mama finally came back out on the porch telling me the yard looked good enough for now and that it was time for me to run on down to the store for a few things. This really got Nell Faye's goat. She was blubbering and asking Mama why she couldn't go instead. Mama just pointed at the churn with one of her own serious looks. Of course Nell Faye knew that meant to shut her yap and keep churning. But she wouldn't give up.

"Mama, let me and Earl D. draw straws, then whoever wins gets to go. Ain't that fair enough?"

Mama looked at Nell Faye, then back to me. There I was with my mouth open, not knowing exactly what to say. Mama spoke up. "Earl D. you want to draw straws with Nell Faye to see who goes to the store?"

I hung my head, finally saying quietly, "I reckon so Mama."

Nell Faye jumped and grabbed the old broom, but Mama quickly took it from her as she said, "Nell Faye, just to keep this fair and square, I'll handle the straw business if you don't mind." With that Mama turned her back as she pulled out a straw from the broom. We couldn't tell what she was doing, but shortly she turned around and announced, "Now, whoever wins goes to the store. The other will have to get on this churn… is that understood?"

Nell Faye was grinning like a mule eat'n briars, so sure that she was going to win and I was sulking like I had already lost. Mama came over to the edge of the porch and made the rules. "OK, who wants to pull the straw?" I just stood there numb. Nell Faye popped up, "Mama, let me pull the straw."

Mama asked her, "Okay Nell Faye, which one you choosing; the long or the short one?" First she said SHORT…then LONG…then back to SHORT. Mama hollered, "Make up your mind!" She settled on short. That meant if she got the short one, then I wouldn't get to go to the store and also I would have to finish the cotton-picking churning.

NELL FAYE ASKED TO DRAW… SHE GOT THE WRONG STRAW

Nell Faye carefully looked at the two straws in Mama's hand and started pulling real slow. Mama stopped her. "Nell Faye, the one you started with is the one you are going to end with, so go ahead and pull it on out. She did…IT WAS LONG!!!

"Yea for my side," I said and let out a whoop. Nell Faye let out a moan as she plopped back down in her chair to resume the churning. I tried to hide my snickering, but Nell Faye saw my grinning and gave me a look that would kill a wild cat as she stuck her tongue at me. I returned the same while grinning like crazy. For once I got her goat pretty good, which was rare.

Mama reminded me what all I was to get at the store then I was on my way. I was still chuckling to myself about Nell Faye loosing out in the straw drawing contest. I couldn't wait to tell this to Snag. That good feeling of beating Nell Faye at her own game was making this little walk to the store even more pleasurable.

I noticed the sun was out nice and bright. Strange, out here in the open you could hardly tell we had such a boomer of a storm last night.

I was swinging the little gallon kerosene can around and around as I plodded through the grass and soft wet dirt on the way to the store. My other fun thing was trying to whistle a tune to match the birds that were everywhere it seemed. I even waded through a few remaining mud holes... now those mud holes were sometimes filled with sharp rocks, so I gauged my steps pretty good.

This big moment of rare happiness was for me being able to get away from the yard-sweeping chore and to escape Nell Faye's tongue wagging all at the same time. I wondered at time if her tongue wasn't hinged in the middle. She just enjoyed so much hollering an' nagging me every little chance she got. It was about all I could take at times. I was glad I won the straw draw. Bless Mama's heart, I knew she thought I needed some relief from that Nell Faye. I knew one thing for sure. If Nell Faye kept up this nagging habit she had, she would end up being an old maid sure as shoot'n. No man in his right mind would want a wife that just yakked all the time.

I was still a little worried, wondering if my pal Snag and his family had made it through that storm last night. I was sure if anything bad had happened to anyone, we would've already been told. I kept reminding myself that I was to get a gallon of kerosene, a box of matches,

SNAG & ME – A FLYING IN A JENNY   19

two sizes of nails and some wood screws and a pound of coffee.

Snag, my best chum in the whole world, kept telling me the reason Nell Faye nagged me so much was because she had been king of the roost until I was born. Surely, I was thinking, she didn't hate me 'cause I was born! Well, she better get over it 'cause as far as I was concerned, I planned on being around a long time, whether she liked it or not.

I picked up my pace for I knew I had to get to the store and back pretty pronto. Papa had already told me we had a lot of work to do. There was the door to hang back up and work in the garden to make sure it would survive through the rest of the harvest time. We had to make sure all the plants were standing. Then we'd have to replant the ones that got knocked over or blown over. The worse chore would be hoeing the weeds around the tomato plants.

DAY DREAMING AND BIRDS SCREAMING

Looking around at the morning sky it was amazing how all the storm clouds had left and how hot it was already. As I trudged along on the rutted road, I was thinking that a nice way to relax would be a cool dip down in Fletcher's creek. I really liked to relax down at the swimming hole, but that would have to wait.

Out here on the road it was just me and all God's wonders. Every now and then I could feel a nice breeze blowing toward me bringing with it smells from the fields and all the wild flowers too. The birds were all singing their happy songs, which was just pure endless strings of heavenly music.

One special critter was the mockingbird. He was jumping from fence post to post like he was following me along to keep me happy singing his little feathered heart out. It seemed to be working. The honeysuckle vines on the fencerow really smelled good too.

As I walked along, I'd wave at some of the folks who were in their fields working and they'd wave back. Yes sir, living in Blanchard Forks even with bad storms was about as close to Heaven as I knew of because I liked everything about it and most of the folks that I knew too. At the moment I didn't even have any harsh feeling toward Bubba Jean Fritzwater, our schoolyard bully. Yep, I liked everybody, even that mouthy sister of mine.

I knew the Good Lord was sure nice to my family and me when He sent my great grandpa and grandma to this countryside many years ago. I did notice some new tracks on the road. Not sure if the motor coach from Bowieville had been through here or not. From the ruts, sure looked like more than one motor coach. I wonder who in the world would be coming to Blanchard Forks? We were so small of a place; I wouldn't think anyone would have any interest in this place except for the folks that lived around here. Oh well, so much for tracks in a muddy road.

MEMORIES OF MR. HANDY HENRY

Remembering what Papa had said before I left, I knew he'd be using a lot of nails just getting everything back together after that storm. Course he was always doing little fix-ups on our little place. He was forever patching up something or making something with lumber slabs to hold our barn and stalls together. At those hard times I would often hear him muttering how much he missed Mr. 'Handy' Henry.

I had to admit, Mr. Henry was really handy around our place. He seemed to know how to do about everything when it came to fixing things and farming. We were real good friends. As a matter of fact he liked everyone. I just wished I could play a harmonica like he did. Maybe one day Snag and me would learn how to make pretty music with those harmonicas he'd sent us.

I always wondered where in the world he might be. Was he still in St. Louis or off to some far away place again? Did he ever think about us very much? I knew we thought of him pretty often. Maybe one day he would come back through these parts to visit us again. This time I was hoping he wouldn't have to sleep in the barn.

MEETING MY PAL 'SNAG' AT MR. FOSTER'S STORE

No sooner had I stepped up on the porch of Mr. Foster's store, I came face to face with my first surprise of the day. My good friend and favorite pal, 'Snag' Galloway, quickly spotted me and began hollering at me from around the corner of the store. "Earl D., get yourself around heah… quick! I got something ta show you that's gonna knock yore eyeballs plumb out!"

I was wondering what in the Sam Hill it could be that he wanted me to see so badly. One thing I knew right off; he came through all that storm okay.

I quickly set my little gallon can down, turned and jumped off the edge of the porch. There he was, standing and grinning like crazy. Even his favorite dog Skip was wagging his tail to beat sixty! I could've swore that Skip was grinning too.

I looked at him up and down to make sure he was okay as he stared at me. "What's wrong with you, Earl

D… don't I look like your old pal? Or some ghost, maybe?"

I answered his funny question, giggling at the same time. "Snag, I was just wondering how you and your family came through that storm last night."

Snag pushed his straw hat back on his head and started laughing. "I tell ya, Earl D., you would've laughed your head plumb off if'n you had'uv seen what we went through. Ma an' Pa had all us young'uns get up and in our clothes. Then, when it started get'n real bad, we all ran out and crawled under the house with all them dogs. When all that hail started hit'n the roof and the ground, we thought we were goners."

Now he was laughing so loud. I couldn't help but join in with him… laughing till my sides hurt. When I thought of all of them under the house with the dogs, my laughing would just start all over again. I could only imagine what a mess that must have been under that porch with all them dogs, the rain, lightening, and thunder.

He continued, "Yeah, I mean it was the biggest mess you've ever seen. Boy howdy, we were all wetter an' dirtier than the dogs an' smelt worse too! They seemed glad to see us but I 'speck after all the hollering an' goings on, they were 'shore glad to see us go. After the worst of the storm passed, Ma got us all out on the back stoop, then made us stand in the rain as we all washed off again. I know it was late of morning before we all managed to get halfway dry and lay our heads down again."

I told him all about our doings during the storm and what the storm did to the barn and all. Then I told him about me and Nell Faye drawing straws…he got a big laugh out of that. He was glad to hear that I had won a small battle with Nell Faye.

SNAG SHOWS ME THE BIG FANCY POSTER SIGN

"Hey, Earl D., nuff 'bout all that storm stuff... it's time to talk 'bout something else." With that last remark, Snag grabbed me by my shoulders and spun me around me so I was facing the side of the store. "Lookee there, Mr. Earl D.! Cast yore eyeballs upon that there poster sign. What'd ya think of that there big ole sign of a thang?"

I had to admit, it was a humdinger, and one fancy sign, all right. It was a big, colorful, poster type sign that was tacked on the side of Mr. Foster's mercantile store and post office. It was for sure something to see too. There were all kinds of red, white, and blue colored banners, flags and the like around the edges. Near the top were Bald Eagles perched atop tree limbs. On the sides were pictures of aeroplanes. In the middle of this beautiful poster was a large notice printed in big fancy letters of silver, outlined in black and red, which read:

24   *Joseph A. Johnston*

*** COMING SOON TO YOUR FAIR CITY ***
MARVELOUS FLYING MACHINES
PILOTED BY WORLD RENOWN AVIATORS
RIDE WITH THESE BARONS OF THE AIRWAYS
IN SAFETY AND EXCELLENT AIRWORTHY
AEROPLANES
* * * $3.00 * * *
FOR A HIGH FLYING
SCENIC VIEW OF YOUR CITY
THIS COMING SATURDAY, 15 JULY
THE EXPERIENCE OF A LIFETIME!
* * * $.25 * * *
ADMISSION AT THE GATE TO SEE THESE
FANTASTIC WORKS OF AMERICAN INGENUITY

About that time Mr. Foster walked out on the edge of the porch smiling as he watched us go on and on about that sign poster. "Hey fellers," he hollered, "What you boys think about that sign?"

We both grinned and told him how nice it was. Also we moaned that it was too bad we wouldn't be able to see this aeroplane show 'cause we were stone-broke.

"Well," he started to explain, "Early this morning three large trucks with tanker trailers come through on their way over to the park. They stopped and chatted for a spell and then asked if they could put this poster sign up. Course I'm always ready for something exciting to happen around here and a 'Flying Circus' should be something pretty exciting to see don't you think?"

I looked up at Mr. Foster and once again we told him how broke we were since I don't think he heard us the first time.

Mr. Foster made a sad look on his face. "Fellers, that's too bad, but now I always heard if you think about something real strong like and the Good Lord smiles on you, then it will happen. But right now I got something else on my mind."

Then we saw his famous smile come back on his face, which meant something else was in the offering.

MR. FOSTER MAKES US AN OFFER

"How'd one of you like to earn a cool soda?" he asked.

We both raised our hands at the same time. We always jumped at the chance to earn a soda or a cookie or even one of those chocolate candy bars with nuts in it.

Mr. Foster pulled a two-bit coin from his pocket. We both spotted that instantly. That was just what we needed, but it belonged to Mr. Foster.

"Okay fellers, we gonna make it fair and square." Then he flipped it in the air and down it came, bouncing around on the old wooden porch of the store. Mr. Foster quickly stepped on it. "Okay boys, one of you call it— heads or tails?"

Snag hollered first. "Tails!" 'Course that left me with 'heads.' Mr. Foster raised his foot slowly as we rushed over to the edge of the porch to see what it was. "HEADS! I got another winner," I yelled as I turned to Snag with a big grin on my face. "See, you don't win all the time, Mr. Snag."

"Yeah, I know, Earl D., but would you kindly let me have just one itty-bitty little ole swig please...purty please?"

"Well, that depends on what I have to do to earn the soda. Now you rascal, if'n I do let you have a swig, you can't hawg it all or slobber all over it! You just wait here whilst I go help Mr. Foster. I'll be right back in a shake."

Jumping up on the porch again, I handed the gallon can to Mr. Foster as I listened to what had to be done. Then he proceeded to draw my kerosene while I did his little job.

To my liking, it was just a simple little chore of bringing three boxes of commodities from the little storeroom in back to the front porch of the store. There, with Snag's help, we loaded them on the Sweeny's family wagon. Strange I thought, there were no Sweenys about!

"Where's the Sweeny folks, Mr. Foster?" I asked.

Mr. Foster glanced around then explained. "Oh, I think it's just Missus Sweeny an' she's over at the church house doing something for Sunday. Not right sure, Earl D. Maybe she's practicing a new song or something."

Thinking to myself, I always thought the Sweeny family sang pretty good at church and more so because their mama was a great piano player. Yep, to my way of thinking they sang pretty good. Not that Snag thought so, but then again, he never offered to get up and sing with them. Instead he would stand there beside me and sing extra loud. This usually upset the Sweeny kids and sometimes the preacher. Then for the rest of the church service it was a staring game between them and him. I just felt it wasn't right that he should complain about their singing and not be willing to join them.

Mr. Foster, just as he promised, presented me with a cool soda pop. I opened it with a bottle opener on the side of the door facing of the store. Awwww, the ever-present fizz it made told me it was going to be some kind of good tasting—especially on a hot day like today. I thought it was a right nice reward for my hard labor I just did… along with a tad of help from Snag.

SHARING A COKE AND JIBBER JABBER WITH SNAG

I ran back out to the porch and of course, Snag was already watering at the mouth to get a sip. "Hold your horses, Snag. I get the first swig. Now rascal, like I said before, you better not slobber all over or gulp half of it down either, Mister!"

Snag just stood there with that silly grin of his, which meant he might and he might not slobber on it, which would usually make me forget about drinking anything after him, even after wiping it with my shirt sleeve! 'Course Mama would have a pure D-fit and my hide if she knew I drank after anybody. So this I had to keep a secret.

We resumed our position on the side of the store where we were once again staring with great intensity at this large poster while sharing that delicious soda pop.

I looked at Snag, wondering what was racing through his head. "Snag, you know after that storm last night, I was really worried about you and your family."

Snag turned with that grin. "Why thankee there pal... we was all worried 'bout y'all too."

"Snag," I asked, "How come you and me don't have more close pals like us?"

Snag scratched his head, "I don't rightly know, Earl D., must mean one of us smells!" Then he started hollering again. I had to laugh too.

"Really, Snag, I mean why it is that other fellers seem to hang around with four or five fellers and then there's just you and me."

Snag got a serious look on his face. "Earl D., you trying to tell me I'm the one that smells and you want

28   JOSEPH A. JOHNSTON

to get in a gang of other folks that smell better and get shed of me as a pal?"

I knew I had put a burr under his saddle. "No, Snag, that's not what I was saying at all. But I just wondered why other fellers hadn't wanted to say, join up and be pals with us too. That's all."

"Well, I tell ya Earl D., that all sounds too cotton pick'n serious for my empty head. What's say let's work on get'n some money so we can go see them aeroplanes."

I looked once again at the large sign with a wishful sigh, knowing it would be another miracle to get enough money to see the aeroplanes. I then quickly looked across the road to the church and then back to my chum. "Snag...reckon where all those Sweeny kids are today?"

"I don't know, Earl D... now shorely you ain't want'n them brats to be chums with us."

I laughed. "Well, we could do worse, you know."

Snag giggled a bit. "Maybe their pa has 'em sweat'n a bit out in their garden." We both giggled knowing we were escaping that chore for the time being.

We weren't sure where the Sweeny kids were. Usually they tagged along with their Mama about every place she went. Maybe the whole family was over at the church house, even though Mr. Foster said he only saw Missus Sweeny. Maybe they were picking up a bunch of limbs from the storm too.

As we pondered the large poster a bit more, out of the corner of our eyes we spotted Mrs. Sweeny walking quickly over across the still damp road, dodging mud puddles as she went. She nodded to Mr. Foster and waved at us then climbed up in her wagon and took off like a herd of turtles, all by herself. I guess Mr. Foster was right the whole time. There were no Sweeny kids.

SCHEMING FOR A WAY TO SEE THOSE AEROPLANES

Well, so much for that. She didn't even say 'thank you' to Mr. Foster or nothing. She must have something terrible fierce on her mind, 'cause most times she'd stop and talk your ears off. I decided that wasn't for me to worry about. At the moment, this poster of a thing had us both into some very heavy thinking and scheming.

One thing of great concern that came to mind, as we both continued studying this fancy poster very closely, was where in the world we would ever get twenty-five cents each to see something such as this aeroplane show at the park? Finally, the silence was broken by my old chum and best pal, Snag.

"Earl D., you ever seen a real live aeroplane? I mean one that you've really put your hands on? No fibbing either!"

"Nope," I answered. "But I've seen 'em in that stack of yellow magazines at school. What'd ya call 'em— the uuuuuuhhhhh—Natural-Graphics or something like that. I heard tell that some folks call 'em 'Flying-Jenny's. All I know is, they must be some special kind of brave folks to fly them things up there with nothing to hold onto, a-chasing buzzards and flying through the clouds. Mercy, just the thoughts about sailing around in the air makes me dizzy."

"Well, tell ya what, Mr. Earl D.," Snag chimed in. "If'n ever I get a chance I'd go ride'n in one. Why, I'd do it so quick it'd make yore head swim!" With that, he turned his head up then began going in a circle, with his arms flung out, kicking up the dust with his bare feet, making a terrible racket, acting just like he'd be lifting off the ground any second. Suddenly he stopped,

30 JOSEPH A. JOHNSTON

then turning his attention back to me—me of course being his main audience—he continued his tall tale.

"Yes sir," he explained in his country boy fashion. "That'll be the greatest day of my life. Well, maybe second greatest day 'sides going to Heaven. Now to let ya' know my heart's in the right place I'd take you along with me Mr. Earl D. What 'cha think about them apples?"

"Tell you what, Mr. Snag," I replied, "You can have my share of them aeroplanes as far as flying in 'em goes. But you know something? I shore would like to see one up close. I don't reckon that's gonna happen anytime soon with my bad luck. Besides, my Papa says if God had wanted folks to fly, He'd gave us all wings. Knowing my Papa the way I do, I doubt if he'd ever let me go near an aeroplane, even if I had a whole quarter!"

"I ain't never seen one of them flying machines either," replied Snag, "'Ceptin' in them books you was talking about. But I'm gonna go see them aeroplanes, my friend, if'n it's the last thing I do...one way or tuther!"

"Well, first mister rich man, where you planning on getting a whole quarter to go to the park? First off, you ain't no magician. Second, you ain't no Jessie James, an' we don't have a bank you could rob even if you were." I laughed.

SNAG'S IDEA ON WHERE TO GET TWENTY-FIVE CENTS

Snag, with his fox-like grin, looked at me with that streak of meanness I knew him to have when he's thinking of something devilish to get us into trouble.

"Earl D., just a hair-brain idea, mind you, but you reckon we could sneak a few cackle berries from yore hen house to raise us enough money to go see them flying machines?"

SNAG & ME – A FLYING IN A JENNY   31

"Nope," I replied. "Mama knows them chickens better than they know themselves. And one other thing, Mr. Snag, we wouldn't get enough eggs in the next couple days to sell to make enough anyway. As a matter of fact, I think Mama must've cast a spell on 'em, 'cause she can tell exactly how many eggs we collect of a day, an' she also knows when an old hen is about ready for the boiling pot. No sir, we can't even think about snitch'n any eggs from my house. Anyway, who'd buy 'em? First thing they'd ask is; 'where'd you young'uns get 'em and does your Ma know you're out selling these eggs!' Nope, we can flat forget that, Snag!"

Snag was stirring his big toe in the dirt, probably thinking of another scheme to get us a couple of quarters for the park. I knew too, his scheming sometimes led us into deeper trouble with our folks. Trying to make sure he didn't get us into a mess with our folks I quickly reminded him that we had to find a way to get the money... honestly.

"Snag, we just got to think of a way to see the aeroplanes without get'n our sit'n down places tore up. So you start thinking of a good an' safe plan an' I will too. The way I see it, unless we play it safe an' do this right, we ain't ever gonna see no aeroplanes."

Snag shook his head in agreement. "Earl D., I hope you know what you're saying, but it sounds to me like we ain't gonna see no aeroplanes if we're banking on your folks or mine to let us have any two-bit pieces. If'n we can figure a way of get'n in there for free an' even if'n we get caught... shoot, what's a little whuppin' when you think 'bout all the fun'n we'd be having."

"Snag, all I can say is... we gotta pray about it and that's it. If'n it don't happen, then we gotta think it was for the best... don't you see?"

32   JOSEPH A. JOHNSTON

I could sense his thinking that I was wrong and decided to call it a day.

Taking the last swig of the soda before Snag could grab it again, I ran around the kerosene tank, tossing the empty bottle toward Snag, both of us just a yelling and carrying on like we didn't have good sense. This hollering and screaming on our brought his favorite dog Skip out from under the store porch, where he had departed several minutes before to find a cool place. Now he titled his head sideways, gazing at us with a question on his sad-eyed face, I guess, wondering if we'd lost our minds, or did we need worming. This dog was totally devoted to Snag and was always right under his feet wherever he went. But when I was with them, he liked me too.

THE TALE OF SKIP'S NAME AND FAME

Chancing a longer story than usual, 'cause I must've forgotten, I bravely asked him how he came to name his dog 'Skip.' Waiting for a normally long spell of Snag's usual story telling about Skip, I was surprised when he said, "That's easy, Earl D. Juss watch this." With that, he whistled to Skip as they started running around in a circle. He would holler "SKIP," and that dog would actually do a funny little hop with his back legs! He'd only do it when Snag would holler "SKIP" real loud. We both got real tickled watching Skip do his little dance.

Noticing the sun climbing into the morning sky I yelled out, "I gotta get going, Snag, with that stuff Mama sent me after 'fore she sends that Nell Faye looking for me. Now you know how mean that older sister of mine can get when she has to fetch me. Besides, I've got some more chores to do an' Papa will be getting a little touchy if I don't get those nails and screws back to him right quick."

I rushed into the store to return the empty bottle and make my order while Mr. Foster fetched me what I came for. Then he put it on the ticket with the usual comments.

"Earl D., thank your folks for me an' I want to thank you too for helping me out a bit ago. Tell your folks howdy an' I'll be seeing you all come Sunday."

"Yes sir, I surely will, Mr. Foster, an' you're welcome on my helping you out. It weren't nothing hard at all. I really 'preciate the soda you gave me too. Sure went good today."

"You're welcome too, Earl D. Now you have a nice day and don't work too hard. It's pretty hot out there in the sun."

I had to giggle a bit. "Well, I'll try, Mr. Foster, but it all depends on Papa when I get back home." We both laughed again.

I grabbed my little sacks of stuff and went back outside where Snag was waiting as he handed me my little can of kerosene. Taking it, I told him thanks and that I was happy that he and his folks made it through that bad storm okay. Snag nodded his head. "Same here, Earl D. Reckon I'll see you a little later on this evening sometime?"

"Sure, Snag, come on over whenever you like. With all I have to do, I won't be going anywhere anytime soon. If we're lucky, we might get down to the fishing hole a little after dinner time."

Snag nodded his head as he replied, "I guess that'll be all right. Reckon I'll see you later on after a bit too, if I get finished with all them chores I know that's a-wait'n on me."

34   JOSEPH A. JOHNSTON

Snag was giggling again. "You think we'll get 'em all done 'fore dark thirty?"

"Yes sir, Mr. Snag, I think we will if'n we work at it, an' thank you kindly for asking, rascal. Why you always reminding me of hard work?" He just laughed.

A LITTLE ABOUT SNAG AND HIS HOME PLACE

With that last exchange and a quick 'bye-bye', I hurried off the porch with the sacks of stuff, hanging onto that gallon can of kerosene, which was already weighing on my hands and arms as I trudged off.

Snag was just getting set to mosey back home too. With a backward glance I was shouting one final important message to him, "Don't forget, if'n we're lucky, we're still going fishing later on this evening!"

"Now Earl D.," he yelled back, "You know, all you gotta do is finish with your piddly little work then we shore gonna do that thang. Ya know juss as shore as the Good Lord made little green apples we're gonna go a-fishing, even if its dark thirty! So, you get whatever you got to get done an' grab your ole fishing pole! While you're at it, why don't cha' dig up some of them good ole stink'n worms from your cow lot? Them bream loves them stinking worms better'n I like nanner pudding!"

Knowing that meant more work for me, I made a final request. "Why don't you come an' he'p me," I yelled. "If'n you did, we could get on with fishing a lot sooner an' you can help me dig for them worms, too!"

He answered in his typical fashion of 'maybe I will and maybe I won't.' "Well, you drive a hard bargain, old friend. I'll ponder that last re-quest, but for shore I'll be over right after a bit an' then we'll get off to some serious fishing. That is, if you ain't gone to sleep under some t'mater bush or something." We both laughed.

He waved one last time, chuckling to himself. Yep, there was something special about my pal, Snag. For certain he wasn't any different than most other fellers around here. But then again, he was. I knew he was about the funniest person I knew of. He could make you laugh even if you were crying. Now if they could find another feller as easy going as he was, that would be a gang of fellers fit for life. I still wondered at times why we didn't have any closer chums, but glad at least Snag and me were great pals.

I pondered that as I was again looking back over my shoulder every now then. He was a typical country boy like the rest of us around these parts. He preferred going barefooted, mostly because he didn't have but one pair of shoes that would fit him, and any others, he couldn't get his feet into. He was what you would call 'tow-headed' and always wearing a well-worn straw hat and hand-me-down overalls, both having seen better days. When he walked he was slightly bow legged. I stopped for a minute and watched him again as he and his favorite dog 'Skip,' in close pursuit. They had crossed the dirt road and were making their way on his favorite footpath that crossed the pastures to his house up on a hillside. He must have spotted me standing there as he waved again. I tried too but had my hands full of stuff.

I could see his home place in the distance. It was a typical old rambling wooden frame house with a partly rusting tin roof, which was pretty common around our community. It was a miracle that that storm didn't blow it away as it sits out in the open with only a couple of trees around it. It could use some white wash paint. Then it would be more like some of the finer farmhouses in our community. Even our old house didn't have any whitewash on it. Papa says the wood would last longer than the paint, so no painting.

Folks sometimes took a lot of pride in their barns, but not their houses. His folks seemed to be happy enough with what they had and didn't seem to worry too much about having a painted house or barn. Snag, sounding a little like my Papa, said that if you ever painted anything once, then you'd have to do it again and again and to him that was just plain too much work.

The Galloway's house sat atop a small ridge known in these parts as 'Hazards Gap.' Don't recollect Mama and Papa telling us where that name come from, but it must have been a dangerous place to live once upon a time.

'Course, any stranger coming upon their house would be in great danger of being swarmed by a house full of young'uns and several pot-licking hound dogs that called the dirt under their front porch home.

NEARLY HOME AND THINKING ABOUT OUR TOUGH TIMES

As I continued walking down the rutted road toward home, I was constantly switching hands with that gallon can of kerosene to ease the strain on my arms and hands. I was pondering my plans of how to some way scrape up at twenty-five cents! I had to giggle at my thinking. I couldn't remember the last time I had even held a two-bit piece in my hand and here I was thinking I was going to get one! As a matter of fact I couldn't recall when the last time I had a ten-cent piece all of my own.

My mind was still spinning though, trying to think about any possible means of getting some money. I was thinking that maybe Mama would let me sell a few eggs if she was properly asked and explained to what I really and truly needed the money for. Now would be a good time for Mr. Armstead to need some spare help in his garden, but that didn't happen either. Even if he did, my folks would make me help him and then not let me accept any money for it. Papa says it ain't neighborly to accept payment for helping one another.

It was a fact of life. Money was a scarce commodity around our house. When Papa did manage to get a few dollars, it was always to buy staples or seed or something to keep us going. Usually, any extra money was to buy us young'uns some clothes for school and maybe a new pair of mail-order shoes from the catalog.

It was always a pure delight to go down to Mr. Foster's store, which was also the post office, picking up that package in the fall of the year. It was like Christmas coming a little early. As a matter of fact, most times we got even less for Christmas. At least store bought stuff!

Thinking about Papa and Mama, it seemed they wore the same kind of old clothes during the week. Recalling how she would laugh telling about our clothes predicament as on occasion she would say, "Yes children, our clothes may be worn and patched a bit, but they're the cleanest in the county!"

For church and special occasions, like funerals and family reunions, there was a reasonable suit for Papa and a dark dress for Mama. She did have some lighter ones for summer. Those were floral design and mostly from sacks of grain that we would buy every now and then. Then once in awhile one of the ladies of the church would offer out a bolt of material. This was won by drawing a number from a little bucket. Now that was always nice to get new material. Sometimes Mama was the winner. Even when she won, she'd share with others.

'Course most everybody else in our little community of Blanchard Forks were all in about the same shape as us, POOR!

There were a few exceptions such as the Armsteads, Mrs. Schnieder, and the Fritzwaters. Mrs. Schnieder was also known here about as Widow Schnieder. These 'rich folk, as we sometimes called them, seemed to always have a new change of clothes several times a year.

'Course they were much better off than most of the families in Blanchard Forks. They had larger farms, cattle, hired help and the likes. They also visited the big stores in Bowieville. The rest of us were plain ole dirt farmers, scratching out of the land, trying to stay alive! I was wondering too if the big storm had knocked over any of their trees or buildings. That would be sad no matter how rich they were.

DAY DREAMING ABOUT A BETTER TOMORROW

I knew exactly what I would do when I got grown and made some money of my very own. I'd buy us all a bunch of new clothes and shoes and outshine the whole county! I even dreamed about buying a big motor car and driving us all over the county so all the folks could see how well off we were. Well, I knew the Bible didn't necessarily cotton to folks wishing things of richness and fancy worldly things, but just a little bit of that didn't seem so sinful to me.

I sat the can of kerosene down again and took another short rest. Daydreaming I thought was a lot of fun. Mostly 'cause it was free and made me think of better times. But for the moment, I was thinking these times weren't all that bad either. I felt like we were pretty well-blessed with all the things we had. Suddenly realizing time was passing on, I knew I better get moving.

I resumed my trek home with my mind racing back to the here and now and just in time as I glanced down, barely missing stumping my big toe on a large pointed rock in the middle of the lane. That would have hurt all day and then some!

Going barefooted had its share of pain and suffering, but most of the time, walking in the grass or loose dirt felt good. One place that wasn't fun walking around barefooted was the cow lot!

I noticed my friend the mocking bird was keeping up with me again as I came down the lane to the house. He sure must be feeling good today with all that singing he was doing.

MAKING MY PLEA TO MAMA ABOUT THE AEROPLANE SHOW

As I made the corner around the side of the house, I heard Mama in the kitchen singing a pretty song that I'd heard her sing many times before. When she was busy and we weren't in her way, she would sing real pretty like. Then she would start whistling. Now that was really wonderful to hear Mama whistle. That meant she was extra happy with life and none of her young'uns were pestering her for something.

I never understood why she and Papa didn't sing in the church choir. Maybe they didn't want to upset the Sweeny family since they had been the singers and piano player as long as I could remember.

Climbing quietly up the back steps, I eased up on the back porch with the kerosene and little bags of other stuff, setting them down quietly. I gazed through the screen door drinking in the home sweet smells of our kitchen, which meant something mighty tasty was cooking on the stove.

I watched Mama for a just a short few moments before I broke her spell. "Mama...Mama," I hollered, causing her to quickly turn around. With a big smile on her face, she motioned me inside.

"Earl D., you trying to spook me or something? What in the world are you so excited about, young man? Are you just now getting back from the store? And... aren't you suppose to be a-hoeing them tomato plants for your Papa?"

"Yes'm," but I had to talk to Snag a minute or two down at the store. She looked at me with that special look. "Now Earl D., you know whenever you bump into Snag it will always take you longer to do what you are supposed to be doing. But, I'll let it pass, just as long as you hurry and get out there to helping your papa.

I knew I better start explaining about what all happened down at the store with Snag and that big poster sign we saw.

"Mama, please spare me just a few minutes 'cause first I gotta talk to you about something real important. I mean, this is earth-shaking important. I ain't never talked about anything as important as this in my whole life I don't believe!"

She stood there still looking at me rather strongly... "Earl D., you didn't answer my first question yet!"

"Mama, I said I bumped into Snag—"

Before I could continue, she replied instantly, "I heard you the first time, honey. You're always late when you meet up with Snag. I wonder how in the world that child can avoid all that needs to be done around his house?"

Now this caused a familiar, but serious, expression to come on her face as she gave me a real eyeball-to-eyeball stare. "Earl D., you haven't been into any kind of mischief down at Mr. Foster's store have you?" she asked.

"Oh, no-ma'am," I stammered, "I just need a little advice on a teeny-weenie little matter an' you being my Mama an' all, I felt you could help me out maybe." My voice trailed off, which I hoped was a cue for her to ask more about my needs. I felt if I stated my case properly, she'd be willing to help if there was a way in the world for her to do so.

"Well, young feller," she began. "Before I hear your problem, here's a few things from me first."

Using her index finger to count off fingers on her other hand, she began. "Now if you're into trouble, your papa will handle that. If you've done something you're sorry for, you'll have to ask the Lord to help you. If it's money you need, we don't have no money trees growing around this house. If you're hungry, it's not dinnertime yet, and lastly, if you wonder if I love you, the answer is yes. Most of the time! Except'n when you are full of mischief!"

With me constantly shaking my head 'no' as she ran through the 'if you're this or that', she stopped talking and gave me one of her special smiles, grabbing me in her strong arms, pulling me up close and with a strong voice of a loving Mother said, "Actually, Earl D., I love you, Little Percy, and Nell Faye all of the time. Now what's your problem, sugar?"

I TRY TO EXPLAIN THE AEROPLANE AS NELL FAYE INTRUDES

"Well," I stammered again, "Mama, you ain't gonna believe what's coming to town this Saturday over at Spaulding Park. You wouldn't guess in a million years!" I said all this in an excited level, hoping to get her attention.

With a twisted look on her face, she looked at me real close. "Mmmmmmmmm, is it that circus full of gypsies coming back to steal all our crops and chickens again?" she asked.

"No ma'am, you ain't even warm...it's even more exciting than a circus," I screamed, to get my point across.

"Now Earl D.," she broke in, "will you kindly get a-hold of your senses and calm down! Explain slowly what you are trying to tell me, son."

Now we had an audience. Nell Faye came into the kitchen to see what I was yelling about. Percy was hanging on the edge of the table with his big eyes staring at me and then Mama. Nearly enough to make me laugh, but I knew I had to keep talking or else lose this battle right quick. I knew I had to watch what I said, or else Nell Faye would be picking on me about wanting to know everything and telling me why I didn't need it. She did this all the time. I think Mama knew she was up to something and reminded her of a few things.

"Nell, you just sit there and keep quiet. This is something between Earl D. and me, and we don't need your opinions for now."

That made me happy to be sure, now I really had to talk fast. Nell Faye just sat there and gritted her teeth.

Gulping some fresh air and trying to compose myself, I started again. "Well, Mama, while I was down at Mr. Fosters' store, getting Papa those nails, screws, the kerosene and other stuff liken I was s'pose to, that's when I spotted Snag an' he showed me this big ole poster sign on the side of the store. But first I had to find out how Snag and his folks made it through the storm last night and it was so funny, but they all made it fine. Mama, you would have snapped a rib laughing at how

SNAG & ME – A FLYING IN A JENNY 43

they went under the house with the dogs during all that heavy rain and hail we had."

Mama prodded me… "Earl D., we're grateful that all the Galloways made it through the storm okay, but tell me again what was it that Snag was trying to show you."

I looked at her and rambled on. "It was a sign telling about some flying machines coming to town over at Spaulding Park on the fifteenth of July, an' that's this Saturday! Mama, you know it would really be a dream come true if'n I could go see them aeroplanes."

This caused Nell Faye to raise her eyebrows and roll her eyes and start to laugh as if to tell me I was crazy for asking such a fool thing.

I gave her a strong look to tell her it wasn't none of her bees-wax and leave this to Mama and me. But she just sat there watching the discussion.

Seeing a slight look of rejection on Mama's face, I kept up my pleading. "I'd dearly love to go see them, Mama…that is, if you and Papa would kindly let me go an' it only cost a quarter."

I rattled the cost off quickly, watching her facial expression for a sign of sympathy, but saw nothing but a frown. It seemed all my efforts were now a lost cause. I'd never get to go see them aeroplanes!

Nell Faye was snickering again at my moaning. My sister seemed to enjoy it when things went sour for me. I wondered at times if she loved me as a brother or did she just like to torment me.

Mama started talking again.

MAMA GIVES ME THE SAD NEWS, AEROPLANES WERE NOT IN MY FUTURE

"Now Earl D., you know money is scarce as hens teeth around here and your papa's not going to let you

44 JOSEPH A. JOHNSTON

go near some old flying machines for fear of you getting hurt or something. You also know you're his right hand man around here and the Good Lord only knows what would happen to us if anything ever happened to you. I hate to put a damper on your plans, but for now I think you best get on out to the garden 'fore your papa comes to the house looking for you. I imagine you and Snag will be want'n to go fishing or swimming later on this afternoon, so if that's the case, then you better get busy."

I must have had the saddest face in the county at that moment. Mama tried to cheer me up a little. "Earl D., before you head to the garden, I want to thank you 'cause I noticed you did a real fine job of gathering up all those limbs and sweeping the back yard this morning."

I smiled and thanked her but knew that wouldn't help me get any money to go to the park.

Mama spoke again with a reminder about WORK!

"I also know if them tomatoes rows aren't looking clean and free of weeds, your papa is going to be upset which would mean you can forget fishing or swimming for a while."

This last exchange pleased Nell Faye as she gave me one of those 'see there, I told you so' looks as she turned and pranced back into the other room. I knew she was snickering to herself 'cause I could see her shoulders shaking. A fine and caring sister I had, yes sir. She really cared about me and my feelings.

I knew it wouldn't make any sense now to bring up the subject of selling a few of them 'cackle berries.' Mama would have only a one-word answer for me: 'No!'

I handed the sack of coffee to Mama, took the sacks of screws and nails and headed out toward the barn. My imagination was working on my brains again as I

SNAG & ME – A FLYING IN A JENNY   45

began thinking about when I got all grown up. One thing I was going to do for sure. I was going to go see all them aeroplanes I wanted to and wouldn't ever worry about hoeing no dag-gum ole garden full of weeds.

My frustration was getting to me as I grabbed the hoe, then leaned on it. I knew I should be heading to the barn and Papa but I stood there as serious thoughts began to get in my head again. My conscience started yelling at me that I should be more thankful for the good life I had. Thankful we even had a garden, a house, a good Mama and Papa, a little brother and a sister, even though she was mouthy most of the time and didn't like me the rest. Sometimes, life just didn't seem fair. Lady luck never seemed to smile on me when I needed it the most.

I looked around at our little farm and noticed one other thing that bothered me. I didn't even have a dog I could at least talk to at times like this. Papa and Mama said a dog was just something else to have to feed and worry with. I kept hoping that one of these days when one of Snag's dogs had a litter of pups, maybe Mama and Papa might reconsider and let me have a mutt of my own. That hadn't happened yet and that was several litters ago!

In silence I strolled out toward the barn with the hoe bouncing on my shoulder and sack in hand. Me and them weeds would do good battle today.

As I walked along, I was taking a long look up to the heavens for a moment at the blue sky with all the puffy white clouds, thinking maybe God might help If I asked rightly. Then a miracle would happen and He'd kindly whisper to Mama and then she'd whisper to Papa. Maybe they would reason out that I deserved this once in a lifetime treat. Heck, them aviators and

46 JOSEPH A. JOHNSTON

aeorplanes may never come here again and here I am broker than a haint with nothing but holes in my pockets and life passing me by!

Feeling like a chicken in a fox race, I accepted this as a stroke of bad luck of the worse kind.

PAPA REPAIRING THE BARN WHILE CHARLIE GRINS

I got down to the barn and there was poor Papa. He was down on his knees beside the barn wall working real hard repairing some planks. He was still pretty upset at Charlie, our one and only faithful mule, for kicking out the side of the barn sometime during the night. It must have been the fear of the storm that caused him to try and break out of the stall. He did what most mules would do... kick up a storm during a storm. I knew Charlie didn't like lightening or fires. He was even skittish around lanterns, though last night he seemed to be glad about us coming to the barn with one checking on him and his cow neighbors.

Papa was mumbling out loud about how he'd like to knock Charlie in the head at times. I knew that'd never happen. Charlie had a niche carved out in our family. He was the only one strong enough to pull a plow or a wagon. I didn't think Papa would ever knock him in the head with anything, no matter how frustrated he got!

You could practically see the smile on Charlie's face as he played the role. He was munching away on some grass that was near the rail fence and every now and then he would raise his head and look at us. I could just see him smiling, if it were possible for mules to smile, while Papa worked to repair the damaged wall.

SNAG & ME – A FLYING IN A JENNY   47

Papa, seeing me standing there, turned and faced me with sweat running all down in his face and his shirt was soaked already.

"Son, did you get the right size nails and the large wood screws like I asked?"

"Yessir, Papa, I sure did, with Mr. Foster's help."

"Did you tell Mr. Foster to kindly put them on the book for me until I get down to pay him?"

"Yessir, I did, Papa."

"All right, just set the sack there by the saw and leave me be, son. Now you need to get on with your chores. In a bit I want you back here to help me with that barn door."

"Yessir, Papa, I'll come running whenever you need me."

I plodded off to the garden to get on with my misery of hoeing around the tomatoes; happy that Papa didn't notice me coming back from the store a little late with his nails and screws!

I grabbed the ole hoe with great intentions of getting rid of a bunch of old weeds as fast as I could. Adjusting my straw hat, I lit into the green devils. Now… this was pure D misery time if ever there was one. I was just hoping to get this done before Mama rang that dinner bell!

PAPA AND HIS GARDEN AND MAMA'S CHARITY

I knew Papa was proud of his garden. He always bragged and compared his plot to others in the community. It was a nice sized garden and provided lots of vegetables and fruit for our table. It was also the means for our canning each year and getting a little extra money when we traded or sold our fresh tomatoes, corn, beans, onions, peaches, apples and watermelons.

JOSEPH A. JOHNSTON

Papa and Mama had strong feelings about charity too. They always gave out some to others who had a need. Mama always set aside some special jars of canned goods that she donated at our annual Christmas service at the church. She would write little prayers on small bits of paper and using some dough paste, stick them on each jar. She always got a lot of 'thank yous' from the grateful receivers of her jams, beans and relishes. Folks really carried on about her labels with the little written prayers too.

ME AND THEM WEEDS DOING BATTLE

Standing there twitching my toes in the warm soil, pondering the job in front of me, no two ways about it, it was going to be a hot day handling the hoe. You would think after all that rain that the ground would be a little damp. Nope, some of this dirt had turned back into natural rocks!

I was thinking what a pleasure it would be to go swimming about now. On a hot day like this, there was nothing like a refreshing dip in the swimming hole down on Fletcher's Creek. I knew that wasn't possible for the moment. Maybe later though—if I ever got through.

Gazing around at the sky I noticed there wasn't one cloud dark enough to indicate a chance for any more rain later on in the day. I just didn't want another booming storm like we went through last night. For the moment, a small shower would be just a wish as I stared at my torment in front of me.

WEEDS! Here I was again chopping away at the green clumps. The clods of dirt seemed to get harder with each whack I made with the hoe. It was a wonder I didn't break the hoe handle.

Bless it all, the stinking weeds seemed to be stronger than iron and stubborn as Charlie the mule. The sweat was running down my face blurring my vision as I zeroed in on one clump of the green tormentors and then another.

It just seemed impossible for them rascals to get this big since I was in the garden a couple of days before doing the very same thing!

I always wondered why the rabbits would eat all the clover and most anything else you plant, but won't eat these stinking weeds! Seems they could get twice as fat eating this stuff and then it would save me a bunch of work, time, and sweat!

Times like this I wished we had some goats. I've been told those rascals will eat anything. Papa said they'd eat the whole garden too, so we didn't have any goats. I knew the Morgan family that lived behind us had several goats and they seem to be doing all right. Maybe Papa didn't want the worry with them and the milking and feed'n.

I guess our two cows, pigs, chickens, a few Guineas and Charlie were enough worries for him. That didn't include the worry with a family, which I know must weigh on his mind all the time. He was a good Papa though. The best in the world as far as I was concerned.

I made several trips to the back porch and the water bucket, dipping out a cool dipper of water, sipping it ever so slowly, then splattering my face with a hand full to cool me off.

This well water was the best in the county. Some say it's 'sweet water.' I wasn't too sure about that, but one thing I did know for a fact. It sure tasted powerfully good at the moment.

SNAG ARRIVES AND SCARES THE WILLIES OUT OF ME

Soon, I'd managed to get the job down to the final two rows. Hacking away at the weeds in the garden was making my hands and arms ache with numbness. To escape the pain somewhat, I drifted off once more to daydreaming about cooler things and places. I faintly heard someone sneaking up behind me, but before I could turn around there came a loud familiar yell!

"EARLLLLLL Deeeeeeee!" I nearly jumped out of my skin!

It was that Snag! There he was, smiling as usual. That wide open mouth in a laughing fit showing his few front teeth with his well-worn straw hat hanging half over his ears. He was grinning like crazy and had his cane pole slung over his shoulder. Beside him was his ever-faithful companion and favorite dog 'Skip.' Skip was wagging his tail like there was no tomorrow with his tongue hanging out nearly dragging the ground! You'd think we hadn't seen each other for days.

"Snag," I yelled, "Why'd ya sneak up on me like that? Scare a person might near to death!"

"Oh," began Snag, "I didn't really mean to spook you, Earl D., juss thought I'd wake you up since ya seemed to have gone plumb to sleep on that hoe handle."

Rambling on, he gave his reason for scaring the wits out of me. "Course I was trying to pertect you 'cause I know'd your Pa don't like for ya to snooze on the job."

With this last bit of jibber-jabber he began his crazy laugh routine again; sounding like something between a mule whizzing and a pig caught in a rail fence.

I was curious about how he learned to laugh like that, but knowing 'Snag' as I did, he wouldn't tell me the same story twice. I would let that pass until I had time to really sort out truth from tall tales. I knew that his laugh was what caused me to laugh a lot.

He was smiling again as he asked, "You get pur-mission to sell any of y'all's eggs so we can go see them aeroplanes?"

I stopped and looked him with a sad look I was sure. "Nope, old friend... Mama wouldn't even consider none of my begging so's that I might be able to go to the park with you. How about you? You get a two-bit piece out of your folks?"

This only caused more laughing on his part and a little giggle from me 'cause I knew he didn't have any luck either. "I tell ya for a naturl fact, Earl D., you an me must be snake bit with all this bad luck of late. 'Course being pore as a snake don't help none, ya unnerstan'. My folks thought I was plumb outta my mind for even ask'n!"

"Well, Snag, that seems to tie the knot on it if'n you ask me. I don't see any way from here how we gonna see them aeroplanes."

GETTING A LITTLE GARDEN HELP FROM SNAG

Starting my hoeing again, I asked, "Snag, how come you never seem to have nothing to do at home? I know y'all have a garden too."

"Shucks yeah," he replied. "An' it's a big'un too!"

I stopped for a moment, then asked, "Well, how do you manage to get away from your folks and come over here so early in the day? You know blame well I won't be through here for a spell yet then it will be a miracle if'n I get through 'fore dark-thirty!"

"Ahhhh scutterbugs, Earl D., it's simple as eat'n fresh apple pie. We rise 'bout four-thirty of the morning in the summertime an' get most of our work done 'fore

52 JOSEPH A. JOHNSTON

the chickens are stirring good. By the time I get the cows milked an' that ole Dominecker rooster has crowed a couple of times, my Ma an' Pa, all my brothers an' sisters doing all the other things, shoot-fire, we're through in no time! Pa always says, if'n you want to be lazy during the day, you have ta rise early in the morning and work. That's what we do."

He scratched a spot on his elbow, pulling up the straps on his well-worn overalls, then pushed the hair out of his eyes, wiping the bead of sweat from his chin, as he continued telling me how they got all their garden chores done way before dinner time. I nodded my head every now and then to let him know I was still listening, although half heartily. I kept on hoeing and sweat'n like crazy and that Snag proceeded to tell me more than I wanted to know.

"Shucks, when we rise early like 'at, we'd be through for the day till chore time at evening tide." Now he was giggling to himself again as he muttered, "An' you know, with just a tad of luck I won't be there for that show either." He giggled again.

I was thinking to myself, maybe my folks and I were doing something wrong, 'cause we got up early too. The difference was, all the help Snag had and all the help I didn't have! Since Percy, my baby brother, wasn't big enough to do too many little chores and that with a lot of grunting. Then there was Nell Faye, my older sister, who thought she was the wiser one, always managed to stay inside helping Mama. That only left Papa and me to do the outside chores.

About that time Papa came around the barn and whistled for me to come help him with that heavy door. I was glad Snag showed up. "Snag, how's about helping me and Papa raise that door back up so we can hurry up with other things and get to fishing?"

Snag looked at me, then in the direction of the barn. "Well, since you and yore Pa need a strong man to help ya out, guess I am the man." We both giggled as we headed to help Papa.

In just a few short grunts we had the door in close, holding it while Papa fixed the hinges in place and replaced the old screws with some new ones. Rising up off his knees, he checked it out as he swung it shut and then open again.

"Thank you, boys, and Snag, we 'preciate your help for sure."

Snag beamed a smile... "Tain't nothin' Mr. McHenry. Shoot, me an' Pa already put our barn doors back on and the roof of the privy too." We all smiled, but knew we were lucky that the storm last night didn't really send us all into the next county and our privy stayed in one spot.

TALKING SNAG INTO HELPING A FELLOW OUT

A bright idea came to mind on how to get the rest of my work done in a hurry and get off to the fishing hole before too late in the day.

"Snag," I blurted out, "You do want to go a-fishing 'fore late in the day, don't ya?"

"Shoot-fire yeah, Earl D. That's what I'm heah for. Tain't no fun if'n you gotta wait all day to get after them bream! Shucks they might juss go ta bed 'fore we gets there at the speed you're going!"

"Well," I replied, "Tain't but one way we gonna get out of this garden any quicker an' that's if'n you give me a hand with chopping the weeds on these last couple of rows of tomatoes. You know I gotta get these chores done or else I ain't never gonna get out of here to go fishing with you or anybody else!

54   JOSEPH A. JOHNSTON

I saw that sour look on his face like he didn't want to hear the next proposal from me. "Now if you really want to go fishing and you want me to go with you, all you have to do is kindly go up to the house, look under the porch, get that other hoe an' give me a hand. We'd get through an' out of here right after dinnertime. If we work hard an fast, shoot we'll probably have a mess of bream 'fore late evening time, if'n they're bitin'."

Snag wasn't one to normally volunteer to pitch in on hard work, but after helping us with that heavy door I felt he would come around. Usually he found a way to wiggle out of work. Since fishing and telling tall tales were also some of his favorite pastimes, this might work out for the best. The thought of going alone with nobody to tell his tales to was overpowering his sometimes normal lazy nature of helping others.

Turning, he trudged up toward the house to retrieve the other hoe while Skip dug out a cool spot under some pole beans to grab a quick snooze before another adventure with his pals, meaning me and Snag.

Without much talking with only Snag's whistling some tune that didn't fit anything I knew, we got those last rows done in record time.

"All right," I said, "let's go to the cow lot and get some of them worms. Then I'll see if Mama's got dinner ready. We'll be off to the fishing hole in a bit. And, if Papa likes our work, we'll be dragging them Bream in by the minute."

DIGGING UP THE COUNTY'S BEST WORMS

Grabbing a shovel from the barn, Snag began his search for the county's best worms. Finding one, he yelled out, "Boy, them rascals are big an' fat, an' the way they smell, whew—them bream'll be coming for miles up the creek juss to get 'em." Snag continued digging around and soon he picked another one from the rich barnyard dirt, dropping it in an old mason jar.

"Yep, Snag, them are the best worms in the county," I replied. "That's why we catch more bream than any of the other fellers. And another reason is 'cause they don't know where our fishing hole is—that is unless you let 'em in on our secret!"

Snag gave me a quick and hard look… "Now Earl D, you know me an' you got a deal. We don't share that secret with nobody. Not even our own pa's," he replied in a matter-of-fact tone.

Trying to soothe him, I managed a comforting line. "You're right, Snag. We gotta deal and it's for life. Tain't nobody gonna ever get that secret out of me, cross my heart an' hope ta die!"

Snag had some more worry on his mind. "Earl D., you come up with a plan on us get'n to see them Aeroplanes yet?"

I had plumb forgotten about even saying I had a plan and so I was stuttering real quick. "Nope, truly I haven't, Snag, but I've been so busy here 'bouts an' I flat ain't had time to see if it was daylight or dark."

Snag dug around a bit more but didn't sound too happy. "Well, I thought you were gonna get somethin' going so's we could go see them aeroplanes. You didn't get none of them eggs to sell, so's we are cooked goose if we don't think of something. You know them aeroplanes gonna be here an' gone an' we'll miss one of the most excit'n things in our lives."

"Sang, I'm trying, but you gotta give me time. You know my folks don't have a sack full of money an' so I got to play it real easy like in order to get any money out of them. From what Mama already told me, it's a lost cause the way I see it."

56 JOSEPH A. JOHNSTON

Snag nodded his head, but I still felt like he didn't believe me. Oh well, if we didn't get to go to see them aeroplanes, it wouldn't be the end of the world. Now to convince Snag of that fact.

MAMA SAVES THE DAY WITH THE DINNER BELL

About that time I heard the dinner bell ringing from the back porch. Just in time to keep Snag from asking me again just what I was going to do about getting us into the park. Like I was full of magic or something.

I saw that hungry look on Snag's face and waited just a few seconds before telling Snag he was welcome to come share some vittles with us. "Snag how'd you liked some good country eat'n?" I had never known him to turn down food; especially Mama's good cooking. So I knew instantly what his answer would be.

With a smile on his face, he was about ready to start slobbering at the mouth as he asked, "What did yer ma cook up good this time, Earl D.? Is it some of them good yams, maybe some fried corn, green-maters an' butter beans with cabbage-slaw an' cornbread?" With his eyes gleaming, I motioned for him to follow me to the house and we'd find out.

Having had him to eat with us on many occasions, but never to the delight of Nell Faye, I knew another reminder about table manners would have to be made known before we went inside and sat down at the table. Sometimes that sister of mine would pitch such a tizzy of a fit that Mama would excuse me and Snag to go eat on the back steps, just to keep the peace.

Nell Faye said it was because she couldn't stand to watch him and Percy both eat at the same table at the same time! But since Percy was family, then Snag would have to go. She often said she'd just soon go eat down at the pigpen with the hogs rather than have to listen to all the noise that Snag and Percy would make.

Strange, I never recalled all that noise. Maybe if she'd just took her time to eat and then leave the table then all would have been well. I think she just liked to complain.

I had to admit neither Percy nor Snag had the best table manners to start with. I know it took some talking on my part to prevent Snag from getting us both dismissed to the back porch like times before.

As we were walking to the house to clean up, I kindly reminded him about eating properly at the table. "Snag now to keep Nell Faye happy, just remember, no eat'n with your mouth open or too full. Else you know where we'll end up eat'n."

He was nodding his head like he would mind his manners. I wasn't sure if Snag was thinking more about food than what I was telling him.

"Earl D.," he asked again, "You think you might take a good guess at what yore ma is whupp'n up for dinner?"

"Well, to be honest with you, Snag, like I said, I don't know what we're having; but you're welcome to whatever it is. But first you gotta wash those hands real good, 'cause you know how Mama is about dirty hands. And Snag, whatever you do, don't dare mention them aeroplanes coming to town! And don't make no crazy faces at Nell Faye or else me and you will be on the back porch begging for scraps!"

HEADING FOR THE TABLE WITH LOTS OF GREAT FOOD

With a final nod of assurance from Snag, we ran toward the house and up the back steps, stopping briefly

58   JOSEPH A. JOHNSTON

at the washbasin. We lathered up our hands real good with the green pine soap, drying them off on an old flour sack used for a towel. Then we scampered into the kitchen table.

Both of us were sitting on the bench across from Nell Faye and Percy. Mama was on one end of the table and Papa on the other end. Nell Faye was about to announce her displeasure of Snag being in the house again when Papa broke the staring game. "Howdy, Snag, nice to have you join us again. I want to thank you for your help with the barn door and giving Earl D. a hand with that hoeing. Supposing you and Earl D. will going fishing after a bit?"

"Oh, yes sir, Mister McHenry. I was most glad to help y'all out. We already got our worms dug an' ever'thing," he replied excitedly. "We gonna catch a sack full today an' then we'll have some nice fresh Bream for supper. Enough for all of us!"

Papa turned his gaze toward me with a smile on his face asking if I'd gotten the tomatoes cleaned up good. I told him that with help from Snag, we got it all done real good. With that, Papa smiled a bit more and said the blessing.

We commenced to eat some mighty good country cooking of fried potatoes, green tomatoes, okra, green onions, smoke cured pork chops, red eyed gravy and hot fresh cat-head biscuits with well-cooled buttermilk! Nothing better in this country boy's eyes.

The best part of it all, for once, Snag minded his manners because he didn't want Nell Faye to start asking Mama to excuse us to the back steps again. That didn't stop her from giving us both the 'evil eye' and if her hard stares would've done any good, Snag and I would've been goners!

GETTING DOWN TO THE FISHING HOLE

Soon, we were fuller than a tick on a purebred black-and-tan hound dog. Finishing the last of everything on our plates, we thanked Mama for the great dinner and asked to be excused, which she did to the sheer delight of Nell Faye. This sudden leaving by Snag and me only caused Percy to start blubbering excitedly, trying to ask if he could go with us, but his mouth was so full, I was probably the only one who understood him. I hated to ignore him but I ran out the door making like I didn't.

I loved my little brother, but sometimes, just me and my pal needed to go fishing and talking our special kind of serious man-talk... this time we'd mainly be talking and trying to figure out how we were going to get to see those aeroplanes.

When Percy did come along with us, he was forever pestering Snag by asking one question after another, trying to get Snag in the notion of telling more of his famous tall tales. This would cause Snag to get to blowing and going on about something that was usually so far fetched that it even had me listening at times. This always pleased Little Percy to no end but would also mean we'd never catch any fish and that would be upsetting. But today was important. We had to figure out a plan to see those flying machines one way or other.

As we scampered out the door, Papa reminded us to be careful and we were welcome to ride ole Charlie if we treated him kindly. Also, he wanted us back in before the shadows fell across the Hansen bottoms. This bottomland was two very large open pastures right across from our fishing-hole on Fletcher's creek. Papa said they were fields that used to belong to some family years back, but now stood empty...except for lots of blackberry bushes, tall weeds and SNAKES!

This land was right in a bend of Flether's creek. Here was where our swimming-hole and secret fishing place was, all in one. The creek was fairly deep in that bend. We had a rope so that we could swing out and drop into the creek. The bottoms were our favorite place where we picked a lot of blackberries during season. Sometimes we'd poke our poles in the bank with lots of bait on the hook and drop them in. Then we'd take our buckets and go pick blackberries. We might just pick some today, but for the moment, we had fishing on our minds.

Fishing was real good here. There were even catfish in there from time to time. But we liked to fish for the Bream and Sun Perch because that's the fish the Bible says you are supposed to eat.

One thing for sure, Mama sure made some great blackberry pies and muffins. So, it was a pleasure to pick 'em, knowing what was in the offering later on.

CHARLIE THE FAMILY MULE AND SNAG'S NEW PLAN

Charlie was a good ole mule most of the time, but once in awhile he'd get real ornery when he had a mind to. Just trying to get a bridle on him at times caused quite a ruckus. Like this morning real early during that storm, he managed to kick out some planks from the barn.

'Course, he could've been spooked by a raccoon or 'possum trying to sneak in and steal some corn from the barn, or get in out of the storm.

Being careful and talking gently to him, I managed to get the bridle on him. I then walked him around to the fence where Snag threw a couple of croaker sacks over his back to ease the pain of bareback riding.

We climbed on board with poles and a jar full of worms and a bucket in case we caught any fish of keeping-size. With a little prodding of my heels in his side, Charlie moved off and we were soon trotting off to the fishing hole, with Skip our ever-faithful dog-buddy plodding along our side.

We dodged several low lying limbs, hoping we didn't get knocked off, 'cause Charlie knew these woods too, but he didn't particularly care about someone riding on his back all that much. He tolerated us and just went the way he would normally go no matter which way you pulled on the reins! He knew where the swimming hole was.

After a bit, we were in the clearing near the bottoms. Snag was jabbering in my ears again about his plans on getting us into see them aeroplanes.

"Now earl D., let me tell you something I was juss think'n 'bout an' you let me know what you think. You see, I got it all figgered out how we can get in there to see them aeroplanes an' nobody will ever be the wiser… an' the best part my scardy cat friend, we won't need no cotton pick'n two-bit piece either."

"Now, Snag, you know what I said earlier 'bout us doing this in a honest way an' rascal you gotta know they gonna be count'n noses over there. Don't forget you can't just walk in there 'cause of that tall fence around the front of that park. Tell me now, just how in the cat's hair are we gonna sneak past them folks that sell the tickets and take the money?"

Snag gave me an instant reply. "Simple as falling off a log," replied Snag. "We get up early like always. Then I'll get my brother to milk the cows. Whilst the dew is still on the ground, I'll sneak over an' fetch you

62 JOSEPH A. JOHNSTON

outta bed 'fore sunup. Slick as a whistle we'll sneak off down to the park 'fore anybody knows we're 'round. When we get there, we climbs up one of them tall gum trees. There we juss sit an' wait till the crowds gather. When nobody is paying 'tention, shucks, we'll just ease down like we were there as a paying customer all the while an' nobody will know any different."

"I don't know, Snag. I'm afraid that plan is for sure too risky an' a sure thing for a whuppin."

I was trying extra hard to dismiss this idea 'cause I knew we'd get into a heap of trouble and then some with his scheme. I had to remind him of another problem of mine. "First off, Snag, tain't no way I'd be able to sneak out of the house without my folks knowing about it. I just think we'd better find another way to see them aeroplanes, or just forget the whole matter. Maybe we do need another close chum in times like this. Maybe three heads would be better'n two."

"All right, Mister Earl D.," he barked in my ear, " We ain't got no other pal an' so you figger out a better way an we'll do it yore way! I 'member you already tell'n me that hogwash, an' here we be, no closer to see'n them aeroplanes than we were last time we talked 'bout it."

Snag grew quiet. I knew he was a little upset about me saying his plan would get us in a jam, which I knew it would one way or another. Now I had the worry of thinking of something to ease his misery. I knew one thing for sure, I didn't want the pains of a whupp'n either when after a bit our folks would find out we had up and sneaked in.

"Just hang on, Snag, I'll think of something yet. You know we would get our rear ends tore up pretty good if'n our folks found out we went an' sneaked in, whether we got caught or not. And if we did get caught,

SNAG & ME – A FLYING IN A JENNY   63

which I believed we would, why Mama and Papa would be so upset knowing we got caught for sneaking into the park without paying, I'd never be able to get over that. And even after the whupp'n, you have to think what Nell Faye would say or do to me for years to come. I'd never have no peace... just think about all that tongue wagging she'd do day after day. Nope, we got to think of another way."

Snag wouldn't let this lie... "Earl D., as smart as you are, you oughta know the pains of a little ole whupp'n ain't gonna last near as long as the pure-D pleasure of see'n them aeroplanes. Shucks, that kind of pleasure would last your whole life an' them some. Shoot, you'd be tell'n your grandkids and even St. Peter 'bout them aeroplanes!"

This caused us both to laugh... but this didn't last long.

Riding along, I couldn't think of anything that would get us into the park without standing a chance of get'n a skinning from Papa or Mama for doing something that wasn't right. Trying to stall for time I replied with a strong voice of assurance. "Don't you worry a tad bit more, Snag, I've a got another plan in mind and I won't tell you about it right now, but by tomorrow I'll have a way to get us in to see those aeroplanes that won't get us both a skinning from our folks."

Snag replied as expected. "Old pal, seems I heard that song before and here we go singing the same verses over again. I'll juss wait an' see what'd ya come up with."

I didn't really know what or how we were going to get to see the aeroplanes and half suspected that Snag knew I might be stretching it a bit, but he said nothing, as we trotted along in a rare silence.

ARRIVING AT OUR SECRET FISHING HOLE

We were coming up fast on the fishing hole. I began pulling back on the reins. Charlie sensed we'd come far enough and stopped. Sliding down off his back, I tied him near some tall grass under a shade tree down by the creek to keep him busy while we fished.

Sometimes he would really let out a hee-haw and bray loud enough to wake the dead if you tied him out in the sun without something to eat or a drink of water. I figured he wasn't such a dumb ole mule after all.

Settling down to some serious fishing, Snag and I watched the bobbing of the floats, each of us trying to snare one rather than waiting till they took the hook and ran with it. After a bit we both managed to catch two small ones, but turned them loose, neither being as big as a hand-width, which we used as a measurement to determine 'keeping-size.'

The lazy evening summer air got us both to nodding off. I would lean back against a tree and Snag was lying over on some tall grass with Skip snoring away right by his side. Now this was the way to fish. It didn't matter if we got a big one or a small one... just the idea of fishing was all that was important at the moment, along with our little catnaps.

AN AEROPLANE FALLS OUT OF THE SKY

We both woke up about the same time, then we got serious about what we came for... FISHING! We were caught up in that fierce competition of who was gonna catch the biggest fish when suddenly we heard ole Charlie hee-hawing like he was being chased by a booger. Then Skip started barking and howling like he was treeing a bear or something. Then he started running around in a circle like some hornets were after him.

About that time as we were looking around trying to figure out what caused Charlie and Skip to act up so crazy like, right over our heads zoomed this flying machine with a loud swooooosshhhhhh, which almost scared us might near to death! Not to mention its effect on Charlie, who was bucking an' snorting like a regular rodeo mule. 'Skip,' who was now howling like he just lost his last friend, ran over between us and was shaking like he was freezing. He was flat scared!

Standing there with our mouths hanging open, we dropped our fishing poles and strained to see out over the bushes and across the creek to see where this 'thing' was going! Not hearing anything else but seeing a bunch of dust fly, we knew that flying machine had done plowed into the ground or into the trees or something!

"Come on, Snag," I yelled, grabbing his arm as Skip started moaning again. We ran over to grab Charlie to jump on his back, but he wasn't haven't anything to do with us for the moment...he just reared his ears back and nipped at us because for sure he didn't want no part of something that falls out of the sky!

Not waiting to ride Charlie, we ran down the creek, looking for a log we knew about that crossed over. We were yakking and hollering at the same time. "Where is it? Where'd it go? Do you see it? Is it out there? Can you see the aeroplane-rider or whatever it is?"

We had never seen anything like this and we weren't going to miss our chances of not seeing it either! In nothing flat we ran across the slick log, slipping and nearly falling in the creek fourteen times, while Skip swam across jerking himself up on the other side, shaking the water off his back, then running to catch up with us.

66   JOSEPH A. JOHNSTON

We all darted through the bushes and blackberry patches getting all scratched up by the briers but not even noticing it, praying at the same time that we wouldn't pounce upon a sleeping snake.

MEETING THE FAMOUS AVIATOR 'CAPT. RAY B.'

Soon we were within spit'n distance of this strange looking craft. It hadn't crashed after all. There it stood. What a magnificent looking flying machine it was too. All painted bright yellow, with two wings and two sitting down places, so it seemed.

Suddenly we noticed this man walking around the aeroplane puffing on a big cigar and cussing loud enough to hear him all over the county! Snag poked me in the ribs as he whispered, "Earl D., I betcha his ma never warshed his mouth out with soap."

I had to giggle. "You're probably right, Snag. I bet she'd give him a lick'n too for all that mouth of stuff he just spit out."

We were both giggling now because bad words were rare around our homes. We stood our ground, but more than a little nervous as we observed this strange fellow in front of us as we peeked from the cover of the blackberry bushes.

With Snag nudging me forward, we were sneaking up closer and closer as we quietly tried not to disturb him, but too curious to stop. We were drawn to this spectacle like a moth to a flame. Now we were just a few feet from this man when Skip began to growl at him and the machine. Skip had never seen anything like this either.

The stranger, hearing Skip growling, spun around quickly and stared at us, spooking us, causing me to stop dead in my tracks, which caused Snag to bump into my backside with a loud grunt. Both of us stood there shaking a bit with Skip huddled between our legs. Yep, we were one brave bunch all right.

The strangely dressed fellow stood there staring at us with that cigar going a mile a minute. He was making as much smoke as a choo-choo train.

Wondering what the man would say or do next, we just stood there like two scarecrows and stared back at him. I wasn't sure who was going to make the next move as he just kept standing there with his arms crossed, sizing us up I suppose. Then we noticed a big grin coming up on his face. He was wearing a crazy looking hat with some sort of spectacles strapped around the brim and a well-worn leather jacket with lots of shiny buttons on it. He never wiggled a bit and still had that big, smoking cigar that hung in his mouth, grinning at the same time.

Finally the spell was broken as he let loose with a long swirl of smoke that he blew out his mouth, then with a loud, rough, gravely, sounding voice, he barked at us, causing us to jump a bit backwards with Skip cowing behind us, still growling.

"Howdy boys," he said. "Reckon I set down a little shy of where I was supposed to. Darn thing ran out of gas! You know, sometimes I think the darn tank has a hole in it. Maybe from some farmer who got a lucky shot at me for buzzing his cows or something."

He let out a chuckle. We did too, but only slightly.

Snag, feeling a little more comfortable now, boldly took a few steps closer, edging right up within arms reach of this bright yellow aeroplane. Looking at this flying machine with his mouth hanging open, he kept repeating, "Would ya look at this here contraption, Earl D.? Can you really believe this thang is for real? A shore

68 JOSEPH A. JOHNSTON

nuff aeroplane right here... right here in this pasture...
a real live aeroplane!"

The fellow was smiling real big now as he spoke
again. "Fellers, I may be guessing, and mind you I don't
know a lot, but something tells me this is the first time
you boys evah seen a aeroplane up close. Is that a guess
or is that a fact," asked the stranger.

"Yessssssssiiirrrr" we both replied at the same time,
not taking our eyes completely off the aeroplane, while
barely glancing at the stranger at the same time. Snag
hollered out again to the stranger, "We ain't never in
our whole life seen no flying machine up close like this
one. Boy, this is some kind of excitement for sure."

WE LEARN MORE ABOUT CAPT. RAY B. AND THE BIG WAR

We were both rambling on between us about this
unbelievable sight in front of us. I am sure the stranger
was laughing at us for sounding and acting like a couple
of monkeys.

He got our attention with his "AHEM." We looked
up at him as he began. "Mmmmmmmm, well, fellers,
time for an introduction. My name is Captain Ray B.
Ricker. Some folks call me Crazy Ray B. 'cause of my
daring feats in this here flying machine. But I'm a pretty
good aviator even if I do say so myself. Now that word
aviator... that means a person with great skill, courage
and just a tad bit more of smarts than the average bear,
so to speak. A person that has the get-up and gumption
to get in one of these things and fly it around all over
the place and bring it back down safely to ground in
one piece. Now I flew a few of these flying machines in
the Big War. That was way over the ocean in the
country of France. Real scary times too, mind you. I

SNAG & ME – A FLYING IN A JENNY   69

Had lots of close calls but never crashed or got shot down, but I did get shot at many a time. The boys on the ground always patched my machine up good and after a strong cup of that French coffee, I was off once again chasing the Kaiser's aviators." He hung his head slightly. Then with a sad tone of voice he told us about the sad side of his adventures.

"Well, some of my comrades weren't so lucky, God rest their brave souls, but that's the difference between being just a feller that can sort of get one of these complicated machines up and off the ground and maybe not returning in one piece, or a good aviator, like myself, who flew these things all over the place without crashing or being shot out of the sky. You see, fellers, wars are not a lot of fun but sometimes necessary because without lots of fellers giving up their lives for us, we'd all be bowing to a king or something worse. Yessir, I'm here to tell you, I love this whole big old country of ours and I'll do whatever it takes to keep it nice and safe for ever'body. As you will also notice on the tail of this old machine I have 'Old Glory' painted nice an' pretty. Don't y'all think it's a pretty nice package of American craftsmanship?"

We were standing still, nodding our heads in agreement with all he was telling us, afraid to move while he was talking. I decided he could tell tales better than Snag, as he let out with another one.

"Now back to what I was telling you a minute ago. You see, lot's of them young fellers over there in the big war had flown in a aeroplane but a few times and then boom, there they were right into the thick of battle. So, surviving meant you had to have a lot of skill and know your stuff, which I did… and that's why you see me standing before you at this very moment. I got all kinds

70   JOSEPH A. JOHNSTON

of medals for my bravery and I earned ever' one of them fair an' square."

We both applauded his story as he raised his hands for quiet so he could continue telling us more about him and his flying machine. "Shucks, you fellers might not believe this, but I happen to know the Wright Brothers personally! Even taught them a thing or two. Course, they were pretty smart to make something fly and all they had to work with was bicycle parts, a little glue, some sticks of wood, and a roll of canvas."

We just stood there with our mouths still open, both of us amazed at what was in front of us and listening to Capt. Crazy Ray B.'s stories. We weren't sure what was truth or just tall tales, but it sounded good enough to us. I know we would long remember the day we met Capt Crazy Ray B. Ricker.

THE LONG STORY IS OVER…NOW HE LEARNS ABOUT US

Again he broke our spell of fascination.

"Now if I might not be too nosey, just who do I have the pleasure of addressing here in front of me this bright and sunny evening? Might you all be a couple of world famous explorers chasing me around the world, or just a couple of lucky little fellers having a good time out here in this beautiful countryside?"

We both grinned real big and looked at him as he stood there waiting for our replies. Snag broke in quickly. "Well, Mr. Capt. Crazy Ray B. sir, my name is Snag Galloway, an' this here feller is my best pal in the whole wide world, Mr. Earl. D. McHenry… an' that mutt there is my best dog in the world, Mr. Skip."

He nodded his head at us as he strolled around in a circle of sorts with his hands behind his back, puffing that cigar like a steam engine again. Then he started walking all around the aeroplane as if he was looking for something, finally stopping in front of us. There was that stare again. I was getting a little nervous, wondering if he was still sizing us up or what when he suddenly broke this spell of silence.

"Well, fellers it's right nice to meet the both of you, and of course your little dog pal there too... uuugh...Skip, you said? I guess I'm lucky y'all found me... at least in one piece. I was really worried 'cause for miles I hadn't seen too many places to set down excepting a lot of corn fields." He was chuckling a little about this time as he continued his tale. "I knew if I sat down in one of them corn fields I just might have a mad farmer chasing me with a shotgun—provided I survived the crash. Just glad I'm here... maybe the Good Lord gave me a tad more of that skill I was telling you about and He might've had a few of his angels watching over me a bit too, ya reckon?"

We both agreed that it had to be the angels and the Good Lord watching over him, else he would have flat hit some of the tall trees around these pastures, not to mention the rail fences.

LEARNING ABOUT THIS WONDERFUL FLYING MACHINE

He continued to strut around in circles, puffing that cigar, which was getting shorter by the minute. He kept talking to us at the same time. "Yep, my fine young friends, I've survived a few crashes before I learned how to handle this machine real good and I've managed to walk away from every one of 'em with no more than just a scratch or two. Never even broke as much as a little finger in all these years of flying. 'Course, my

72   JOSEPH A. JOHNSTON

appreciation for all these narrow escapes I have to give credit to the Good Lord for guiding me through some tough times and the skills to do so. That's why I call this little plane Angel Wings." Then he proudly showed us for real some wings painted on the side of the plane and the words "ANGEL WINGS."

He started talking again. "My dream is to please many a folk with my type of flying skills before I get to the big hanger in the sky. With just a little luck I can do this kind of flying for a few more years 'cause I'm good at it an' folks that know me, know that too."

Course, neither Snag nor I knew who the Wright Brothers were and guessed he meant that God had set aside a special place for aviators in a big hanger, wherever that was, rather than Heaven. Might be fun for a while, I was thinking, but I believe I'd rather get on over to Heaven if possible.

He watched us closely, then asked, "Now, looking at you lads, I take it y'all might be a tad curious about this heah flying machine and how it works; is that correct?"

"Oh, yes sir," we replied in one voice."

"Well," he replied, "Let me show you a few of the basic things about this fancy flying machine."

With that he proceeded to show us the propeller, and then the large engine up front. Next he showed us where the gasoline was stored, then some parts of the aeroplane he called the rudders, elevators, and clock looking things he called 'gauges' inside the place where the aeroplane driver sits. There were some pedals of sorts and this stick of a thing in the middle of the floor he pointed to, telling us, "Now fellers, these gadgets here are the main devices that I use to make the plane go up and down, turn in a circle and so on. The top gauge there keeps me from get'n lost... it's called a 'compass.' Now see that lever of a thing over there?"

We were both straining to see as we had climbed up on the side of the aeroplane, both struggling not so slip and fall at the same time as Capt. Ray B. continued. "That thingamajig is called the throttle and that's what makes the engine run fast or slow. This part where I sit in the aeroplane is called a cockpit.

We were in a blur trying to see everything and remember too all what was being told to us. I was so excited about being able to climb up and look down into the cockpit place. Snag was rushing me so he could climb back up and look some more too. What a day this was turning out to be.

Capt. Crazy Ray B. got our attention again. "Fellers, have y'all evah flown a kite before?"

We both told him quickly how we made homemade kites and flew them all the time during the windy months of March and April.

He looked down at us again with that grin while taking another puff off of his cigar, which was looking like a stub about ready to burn his lips. "Now if you've evah flown a kite, then this heah aeroplane is nothing more than a fancy kite without strings but with an engine to make it fly off into the God's blue skies."

Seeming pleased with his instruction and settling our curiosity about his aeroplane, which he could easily tell from our wide open mouths and wide-eyed expressions with bits of ahhhhh's and oooooohs thrown in to show our excitement, caused him to grin real big. I guess he realized that he had made a couple of pure country boys very happy with all his tales and showing us his flying machine.

74 JOSEPH A. JOHNSTON

CAPT. RAY B. MAKES US A GOOD DEAL

He next made a proposition that we couldn't resist. "Say fellers, if you two would do me a big ole favor, I'd kindly reward you for your trouble; that is if you're interested in maybe seeing our air show day after tomorrow." Then he leaned back against the aeroplane, watching for our predictable reactions to a possibility of seeing the show.

"Yes sir...we both jumped in front of him. What is it that you want us to do Capt. Ray B. sir?"

"Well, sir," he started, "Do you boys know the location of a place called uuuuhhhh...Spaulding Park, anywhere around this part of the country?"

Both of us yelped at the same time. "We shore do!"

"Well," he said, "My chief mechanic, 'Sparks' Einberger should be over at the park by this time with his trucks and some other fellers that go around with us from place to place. Well, I'm more than certain he and the boys should be there by now. Anyway, they help take care of the aeroplanes to make sure everything is A-OK. There's two of us aviators in this show by the way. So they have to worry about getting two of these flying machines ready for every little show we put on."

We were standing there waiting to hear what he wanted us to do, but sounded like he was getting on with telling us another tale of his.

"Now like I was saying, Sparks has some gasoline for our aeroplanes in a tanker trailer sort of thing at that park of a place. What I want you boys to do is to go over to the park and find Sparks, then lead him back here with some gasoline. How far do you have to walk from here?"

"Oh," I yelled. "We don't have to walk just a tad 'cause we got a mule an' we can ride over there in nothing flat."

He was smiling real big now. "Hey, that's just great. Maybe with a little gasoline, a couple of prayers and a little luck I can try and get this aeroplane out of here before dark and without crashing into a tree. Think you two could do that little chore for me?"

"Oh yes sir," I chimed in. "We'll go fetch our mule right now an' head him over there to the park. Shootfire, we'll be back 'fore ya know it!"

Capt. Ray B. looked at us with a grateful smile. "Well, I'm much obliged to you boys. Now you best get going 'cause it's gonna take a spell for Sparks to get his old bones moving; especially knowing it's me he's having to fetch out of trouble again!" He let out a loud spat of laughing. Now red faced from all that hard laughing, he turned to us again.

GOING FOR HELP FOR CAPT. RAY B.

"Now boys, just one word of warning. Ole Sparks is an ornery sort of ole coot at times, so don't let his bark scare you off with his rough voice. He's just a lot of hot air, totally harmless. So don't let his ugly looks bother you either."

We were giggling and trying to head toward Charlie at the same time, nodding our heads again and again. We'd have to stop in our tracks as he would say something more. Then he said something that got our interest up a lot more.

"Oh, and one more thing. He'll probably have his grandson with him and you fellers will have to make sure you meet him too. His name is Chris. Now let me tell you, he's a sharp little shaffer too. Even though he's young, I think he's smarter than his grandpa on a lot of things! I'm guessing he's pretty close to you fellers ages."

We laughed and said we'd be watchful of Mr. Sparks and we'd look for Chris too.

With that, he laughed at himself and was once again puffing away on his cigar, which was about done. There was just a little stub hanging to his lips like it might fall at any moment. Sure looked funny to me. We made a mad dash as we ran off to get Charlie and head him toward Spaulding Park.

We were both realizing we had run upon a golden opportunity to maybe see the aeroplanes show after all. The best part, we could do it without snitching eggs or sneaking into the park without paying. That was one worry off of my mind. Now I wouldn't have to come up with something to please Snag. Most of all, not get'n a licking for doing something devilish!

Getting Charlie calmed down enough so we could climb upon his back was no easy task, but at long last we were on his bony back and pointed his nose toward the house. I was sure he was thinking of home and so he trotted at a good pace. This mule was thinking the barn would soon be in sight, then he could call it a day. We were thinking of something else.

We were both bouncing, hitting his backbone with our sitting down places, which was starting to smart a bit. It felt better when he just walked. This trot'n could mean a sore sitting down place later on.

In no time at all we were coming up the pasture that normally leads to our home and the barn. As we tried to turn Charlie toward the park, he had other ideas. Charlie had it in his mind to go home and that's where he was headed till we both started hollering, using our feet, ankles and legs to make him turn down the back fence row that would lead us past Snag's place and to the park.

'Course, Skip was running ahead barking as if to lead Charlie and that might have caused him to change his mind. Skip was one pretty smart dog.

ARRIVING AT SPAULDING PARK

After much frustration fussing with this hardheaded mule, we soon rode up to the park entrance. Sure enough there were some large motor trucks the likes of which we hadn't seen too often in these parts. These had to be the ones that Mr. Foster was telling us about earlier this morning. We noticed some tents set up with several men gathered around a campfire that had a coffeepot hanging across it. You could smell the coffee brewing, which smelled pretty good after all that cigar smoke from Capt. Ray B.

To me it seemed late in the day for coffee since we mostly smelled it early in the mornings at breakfast time. I didn't drink coffee but it did smell good in the evening air. It even caused a pang of hunger to hit me.

Snag barked up, "Boy day, that coffee brewing on that fire makes me hongry as a bear cat... I'm slobbering at the mouth thinking 'bout something to eat."

78   JOSEPH A. JOHNSTON

"Well, Mr. Snag, I'd 'preciate it if'n you'd kindly not slobber on me!" He just laughed.

Charlie was balking at the sight of the strange looking machines and people. He was getting more skittish by the minute, throwing back his ears. I knew he was about ready to turn tail and head back toward the house if we didn't try to calm him down quickly.

We scampered off his back real quick, with me hanging on to the reins for dear life trying to sooth him down a bit. With Snag's help, we finally got him calmed down and tied to a hitching post facing away from all these strange sights and noises.

Looking around, we decided to walk into where all the men were gathered, both of us looking around for an old man with aching bones.

"Wonder which old coot it is, Earl D.," Snag blurted out.

"I don't rightly know, Snag, but you could go over an' ask one of them fellers over by the campfire."

SNAG MEETS *SPARKS* EINBERGER

As Snag headed toward the small group around the campfire, I eased back to the hitching rail and tended to Charlie and skip while Snag proceeded with the business at hand. That Snag was strutting around the campfire like he owned the place. He had his hands tucked in his overalls, straw hat pushed back on his head, then when he got close to one of the fellers who were now eyeing him, he yelled out pretty loud like, "Hey Mister, where's the old coot named Sparks?"

The men and one young fellow that were standing around the campfire all turned toward Snag and then broke out laughing like crazy. Well, all except one. I knew now that 'Snag' had hit a nerve with at least one of them. Just as I was wondering what was going to

SNAG & ME – A FLYING IN A JENNY   79

happen next, it did. This older man with graying whiskers strolled over to where Snag was standing, still looking around like he was the president or something, grinning like a mule eat'n briars.

With a grizzled look on his face, the old feller looked down at Snag with an evil eye. "I'm that old coot you looking for, sonny boy, and 'fore I snatch a knot in yore rear, where'd you learn my name anyways?"

Now this pretty hard talking from this old gent caused Snag to do a double take as he stumbled backwards a few steps, gulping in some fresh air and trying to grab a bit of bravery at the same time. "Uuuuuhhh," he began sputtering his words, "Mr. Captain Ray B. told us to come fetch you Mr. Sparks sir, 'cause he told us to come tell y'all that his aeroplane run plumb out of gas an' fer you to follow us over to the bottoms an' bring him some gas real quick like so's he can fly that aeroplane of a thing out of the pasture 'fore dark."

Snag was pretty shook up I could tell from that first meeting with Mr. Sparks Einberger. He was all out of breath trying to say anything as fast as he could to prevent any further encounters with this rough-talking grandpa of a fellow.

With that, Sparks Einberger became like a wild man. He pulled off his greasy cap, throwing it to the ground then stomping on it, cussing and running around hollering so everyone including the Lord must have heard him.

"I knew it, I knew it, that daggum crazy Ray has never gotten to anyplace like he's supposed to! He's always dropping down in some stinking cow pasture and then we gotta go help him out! If that don't beat all!"

He kept circling the campfire, kicking up the dirt and looking rather strongly toward me and Snag, who

80 JOSEPH A. JOHNSTON

was back peddling pretty good about this time. Even Skip was hiding behind me again, with his usual low growl.

Snag eased back over to where I was standing. I nudged him. "Why don't ya ask the old coot if'n he's gonna follow us or not. If he don't, we don't get no reward for helping Capt. Ray B., an' maybe a chance to come to the park on Saturday."

Snag turned around and looked at me like he had done had all the tongue-lashing he wanted for one day. "Lookee, Earl D., I done did the hard part juss get'n him to at least think about going. Since we be partners in this mess, why don't you go finish the job?"

MEETING CHRIS FROM TAMPA

About that time the young fellow we saw standing with the others fellows ambled over toward us with a big smile on his face. "Hi fellers…looks like you all put a burr under my grandpa's saddle. Maybe I can help you with your problem… or I should say, help that rascal Capt. Ray B. This caused all three of us to giggle a bit.

We both looked at him and then Snag blurted out, "You're right 'bout that 'cause I don't think he paid no 'tention to what I juss asked him."

I then chimed in with my bit. "You must be the feller named Chris that Capt. Ray B. was telling us about."

"Yep, that's me in person—not much here mind you, but still it's all me."

He was grinning now and turning slightly, pointing a finger toward the group of men as he continued talking to us. "That old feller who's kicking up all that dust over by the campfire is my favorite grandpa. His real name is 'Gus' Einberger, but since he works on these aeroplanes all the time, they call him Sparks for short. Like a nickname, you know."

We nodded our heads 'cause we knew what nicknames were. Snag was proof. Chris started laughing again. "There's a tale behind Grandpa's nickname and I'll have to tell you about it bit later if we have the chance."

We both looked at him and smiled, in hopes that he might help us get his grandpa moving toward the bottoms before it got any later in the day.

I spoke in his direction. "Chris, it'd be a mighty big favor to us if'n you could talk your grandpa into get'n a move on if he's gonna go at all. We made a promise to Capt. Ray B. and I don't know about you, but us, that's not right to make a promise and not keep it."

Chris spoke up again. "Now fellers, I'm with you all the way. You're right, when a person tells someone he's going to do something, then that's what should happen. Now when my grandpa cools down a bit, I am sure he'll reconsider what you asked and go help Capt. Ray B. No matter what he got into, Grandpa has always went to his rescue in past times. Now I know he talks sort of rough, but most times he's harmless. I got to admit too, he does get a tad upset when he hears bad news, an' let me tell you, when he hears about Capt. Ray. B. plopping down in another pea patch someplace, that's always bad news to Grandpa. It seems about every place we have gone to here of late, Capt. Ray B. manages to do something to cause him to plop down in some cornfield or cotton patch. Then Grandpa and Big Jim—that's the tall feller standing there with that tin cup in his hand—they have to go check it out real good and make sure he didn't cause any damage to the aeroplane bouncing over plowed fields as he has in the past. You see Grandpa knows that other folks will be

82   JOSEPH A. JOHNSTON

riding in the aeroplanes as well, and so he has to make sure everything is okay."

CHRIS, THE AMAZING BOY FROM TAMPA, FLORIDA

I was amazed at how this young short fellow could go on and on talking like a grownup and all. Some of his remarks about his grandpa and Capt. Ray B. got all of us to giggling a little bit. This new fellow was close to our age I suspected and I was glad he came over. He seemed like a fellow that enjoyed life and funning a lot. I knew one thing after watching Snag's meeting with Mr. Sparks Einberger, I was dreading to try and talk to him about anything.

Chris looked at us both. "Well, you fellers know my name and I don't know yours."

Snag jumped in quickly as he reached out to shake Chris's hand. "Howdy, Chris. My name is Snag Galloway an' this feller here is my best pal in the whole world, none other than Earl D. McHenry. An, that mutt over yonder by the mule is my favorite dog, an' his name is Skip."

Chris looked at us and smiled. "Hey, I like them names and that name Snag…gotta mean something special too, I bet." This caused all three of us to start giggling again. I guess Snag took it to mean a compliment. Course he could have been called worse things I'm sure.

Chris walked over and petted Skip, who liked Chris right off the bat. Normally he doesn't cotton to strangers too well. He must know more about Chris than we did at the moment. Then he patted Charlie and it was another amazing feat. That Charlie didn't throw his ears back like he normally does when you try and pet him. That Skip was right under his feet wanting more petting and scratching his head as he was wagging his tail to be sixty.

Chris walked back over to where we were still watching the folks around the campfire, wondering when Chris's grandpa was going to get some gas and follow us. "That's a nice mule you have there, Earl D. and Snag, I like your dog too. I got a dog back home. Boy I'll sure be glad to see him and my folks again. I miss them a lot out here so far away from home."

I looked at his face to see a bit of sadness as he was again rubbing Skip's head. "Chris, I know you miss your folks a heap. I don't think I could take off and leave my folks very easy. Now I have a sister who would probably be glad for me to up and leave at times."

Chris started smiling again. We were just standing there shuffling, thinking maybe Chris had forgotten that he was going to go talk to his grandpa. I poked Snag and he nudged me back trying to get one or the other to go talk to this *Sparks* Einberger. I was a more than a little uneasy about it, but we finally got a blessing from Chris; seeing our uneasiness, he kept his promise.

CHRIS COMES TO THE RESCUE

"You fellers don't worry. I know you need some help talking to my old stubborn Grandpa and I'll help you out if I can."

I blurted out quickly…."You bet, Chris—that is if you think you can get your grandpa to go with us to fetch Capt. Ray B. out of the bottom-lands, cause it's get'n late of the day. We'd be much obliged for sure."

Chris motioned for me to follow him. I turned to Snag.

84 JOSEPH A. JOHNSTON

"OK, Snag," I said, "Watch Charlie whilst I go with Chris to try to talk to Mister Sparks." That rascal Snag smiled sneaky like and raised his hand and waved a tiny bye-bye to me. I'd get him back one day.

I began edging over near the group of men where Mister Sparks was still fuming, but at least he had his hat back on his head. I waited until Chris made a move to talk to him.

"Grandpa...?" The old fellow turned with a jerk, still wearing a scowl on his face like he didn't want to hear anything from anybody. Chris must have known how to talk to his grandpa under a bad situation, as he spoke to him again. "Grandpa, this feller here has something he needs to talk to you about an' I think it's mighty important that you listen up. Okay?"

TALKING WITH MR. SPARKS EINBERGER

Mr. Einberger didn't seem too interested in hearing anything from anybody. Just as I was about to turn and head back to Snag and Charlie and call it a lost cause, he turned and looked my way, I guess to listen to what I had to say. I was nervous as a cat on a hot tin roof about this time. He was giving me a pretty hard look, so I looked him dead in the eyes-balls too. Papa always said it was the only way to deal with hardheaded men or mules. I managed to finally get my tongue untangled as I wanted him to get him going.

"Mr. Sparks sir, I know you're upset an all, but if you'd kindly get some gas for Capt. Ray B. an' follow us, we'd be right glad to lead you over there to where he's sitting in Hansom Bottoms. But if'n we wait too long, we'll have to leave 'cause I need to get our mule back to the barn. Then poor Capt. Ray B. will have to stay all night out there in them lonesome bottoms with no food,

SNAG & ME – A FLYING IN A JENNY   85

no one to talk to 'cept'n hoot owls an' then maybe getting scared out of his wits by some ole boogers or wild cats that prowl around in the night and scream a lot."

He turned around looking down at the burning embers of the campfire, then back at me, staring what seemed like several seconds, which only caused me to get more jittery. He let me know what he thought about all my fears for Capt. Ray B.

"Well, maybe a night out there in the dark woods would do him good. Maybe he'd learn to get to where he's supposed to without plopping down in a pea patch someplace."

Just when I was dreading that he might not go at all, Chris came to the rescue again.

"Grandpa, you know he didn't mean to plop down on purpose. Besides, you know we have to have his aeroplane here first thing tomorrow so you can check it out and make sure everything is okay with it. If we don't help him, then that's gonna make this a bad show for sure."

Those were the magic words. Mr. Sparks stared at Chris then spoke. "Chris, you're too smart for me. You're better than your mama at making me do things I don't want to do. You know all the reasons to help him out and I can only think of many reasons not to. So, I guess you win again. I'll fetch some cans and pour up some gas for that rascal… just this time and never again…I swear it!"

With that he stomped off toward a tank of a thing on wheels, which was hitched to one of the large trucks they had. Chris and me trotted in behind him as Chris gave me a wink. "Earl D., I think he's going to go with you." I looked at this young fellow with the big smile on his face. I shook his hand real hard. "Thanks, Chris,

86   JOSEPH A. JOHNSTON

you really know how to work your grandpa and now our promise to Capt. Ray B. will work out just fine."

LEARNING A BIT MORE ABOUT THIS FELLER CHRIS FROM TAMPA

Chris just smiled. "Well, I'm getting a lot of practice."

I had to laugh again. Now I was thinking, this young feller would sure make a nice chum for me and Snag. Only problem is he'd be leaving when these folks left. That would be tough just meeting a new chum that you liked a lot and then they leave like a wisp of wind. That's sad to even think about and we didn't really know him good yet.

As we walked over to where his grandpa was gathering up some large metal cans I asked another question. "Chris, where in the world do you live?"

He smiled but then a sort of sad look sprung up on his face, but just as quickly, he laughed it away. "I live in a place way down south of here called Tampa, Florida."

I noticed straight away, he had a nice chuckle like he was mostly full of happiness all the time and never let sadness rule him. I wished at times I was like that. 'Course I had an aggravating sister that kept me upset a lot. Maybe Chris didn't have a sister. That could be a blessing, I was thinking, especially if she was anything like Nell Faye.

That thought caused a bad feeling rather suddenly. My conscious was whupp'n me good for those thoughts. I knew Nell Faye loved me; she just had a funny way of showing it. I knew too if I didn't have Snag for a friend, my world would be pretty sad and empty. I'd have no one to shoot marbles with, go fishing and swimming with. I knew good friends last a lifetime and if the Good Lord was willing, that's the way it would always be between Snag and me. Now if Chris lived around these parts, the same would go for him too.

Chris looked up at me as he began telling me more about this place where he lived and all. I noticed he was just a tad shorter than Snag and me, but that was okay. At least he didn't have the nickname of 'Shorty'.

"Earl D., where I live is real nice. We even have oranges trees right in our back yard. As a matter of fact when they come in season, shoot we just go pluck one right off the tree. Yep, it's quite a good life if you happen to live in Tampa, Florida."

I stood there nodding my head, but I didn't have any idea where Tampa, Florida was from here. I just knew that according to Chris it was way south of here by a long ways and then some. I would have to look at some books with maps one day and find this place called Tampa, Florida.

"Wow, Chris, what's it to do down there in Tampa, Florida?"

"Oh, Earl D., you and Snag would really like it. Shoot, it's summertime nearly year round down there. Also, we're right near the ocean. You can go down and walk in the ocean and it has pretty white sandy beaches as far as you can see."

"Oh boy, that sounds like a nice place all right," I replied. "Well, sort of nice. If it's summertime all the time, then that would mean having a garden all the time and that means work. I think if it's all the same to you, Chris, I'd just soon stay here. At least in the winter time we don't have to work in the garden."

He laughed at me again as I asked more questions.

"Mercy, I bet it took y'all a long time to get here to this little wide place in the road, didn't it?"

88 · JOSEPH A. JOHNSTON

"Oh, it don't seem so long. We only stay in a place for a couple or three days and then we're off again. When it gets close to the end of summer, Grandpa will be putting me on a train and I'll be heading back home."

CHRIS THE BRAVE TRAIN TRAVELER

"You mean all by yourself?"

"Sure. There's nothing to worry about. I already know where to change trains and all that. I'm a good reader and my folks are good teachers. Before I left, they taught me all about train schedules and the like. So, it won't be a problem. Shoot, they've taught me so much, I bet I can find my way to heaven too!"

"Mercy, Chris, all I can say is that you're a mighty brave young feller to be traveling around by yourself. Yeah, you mentioned get'n to heaven an' all. It might be a tough trip for some folks according to our preacher, but the way he yells at us 'bout being good. I'm sure St. Peter will fling those pearly gates open wide an' welcome us to heaven 'cause he knows the preacher has scared the devil out of us, tellin' us a million times that we best be good or else!"

Chris giggled a bit, then smiled again as he told me about his traveling plans. "Oh, I won't be alone on the train. I'll meet lots of nice folks and I'll have my books and checkers with me. So when I'm not reading I'll find somebody to play checkers with me. You know you can meet some mighty nice folks on the train. It's easy to be sociable, if you talk right and listen too. It's just a fun thing to do. Most folks I've learned like to play checkers and tell tales. I'm pretty good at checkers too. I let them win the first couple of games and then I'm on the attack and beat them till they holler uncle!"

Now that got me tickled for sure. I could just see him beating some old feller at a game of checkers.

WATCHING SPARKS EINBERGER POUR UP THE GAS

We gathered around his grandpa as he was getting ready to fill those cans with that gasoline stuff for Capt. Ray B's aeroplane. His grandpa turned toward us. "All right, you two, don't be lighting up no matches or else we could get blown plumb to glory!"

This scared the willies out of me as I was getting ready to high tail it out of here…gas or no gas! Chris grabbed my arm, drawing me back to where we were, laughing at the same time. "Hang on, Earl D., we ain't get'n blowed no place." Now he and his grandpa were laughing at me. I tried to smile, but was still a little nervous.

When I got settled down, me and Chris resumed our talking. Just listening to him was so interesting to me to what all this young feller could do…all by himself.

Chris looked my way again. "You ever play checkers, Earl D.?"

"Oh yeah," I replied. "I play that all the time. I don't win all the time like you, but it's a lot of fun. Me an' my papa play sometimes when he ain't too busy. Once in awhile I can even get my older sister to play, but she gets a mite upset when she loses. I call her a sour head at those times. Sometimes I have to play all by myself 'cause Papa and Mama are mostly too busy and my little brother Percy don't know how though he would like to learn. Yep, I really like checkers, Chris."

I then saw a sly expression come upon his face, which told me he was a fox at getting you into his pocket, so to speak.

90 JOSEPH A. JOHNSTON

"Earl D., how about a game called *Chess?*" he asked.

I was scratching my head real good, but I had never heard of game called 'chess'...."Nope, can't say that I have, Chris. At least in these parts. What ya gotta do to play this game you're talking about?"

"Well, Earl D., it's a little complicated to explain. Wish we had more time and I'd show you better than I could ever tell you. You use a board just like the board you play checkers on, but you have a whole different set of figurines to use and the moves are a lot more complicated. Anyway, someday, you need to read up about the game of chess. You and Snag would be kings of your school if you were the only two that knew how to play it."

"Chris, I'll do my best. Sounds like it may be fun."

"Well, maybe not fun so much, unless you win. One thing for sure, it makes you think a lot. Folks usually use the word 'strategy' when you talk about that game."

"Shucks, Chris, there you go using them big dollar words and I don't have five cents worth of smarts between my ears."

"Not to worry, Earl D., you're plenty smart… you just need to see and do a few more things, and you will too one of these days real soon I'm certain."

CHRIS WOULD MAKE THE WORLD A GOOD FRIEND

Now I knew instantly Chris and me would be great pals 'cause we both liked Checkers and here he was trying to tell me about another game called 'Chess'.

We stood and watched Mr. Sparks at this tank of a thing as he finished with one large can. Now he was taking the other metal can and began to fill it up with this stuff out of that tank.

Mercy, did it smell ever so powerfully strong. It smelled even stronger than the kerosene down at Mister

SNAG & ME – A FLYING IN A JENNY 91

Foster's store. Thinking to myself, no wonder aeorplanes could fly if they used something that smelled that strong! I hollered at Chris... "You know, Chris, I was thinking if a buzzard took a few sips of that stuff, he could fly to the moon and back."

We both laughed out loud. Now I could understand how it might just be powerful enough to blow us to glory like Mr. Sparks Einberger said.

Turning back toward us after he finished filling the second container, Mr. Einberger, with a heavy frown on his face, barked out, "All right, you young whipper-snapper, if think you can lead us out there wherever in tarnation that crazy jackass plopped down at, we'll follow you. And, let me tell you here and now, you and that other squirt better be telling us the truth 'cause I don't take too kindly to folks who waste my time, or lead me on a wild goose chase! You understand what I'm a saying?"

I nodded my head in a silent, fearful, understanding.

Chris came over to my side and sort of gave me a comforting smile. "Earl D., he ain't really mean. You just lead him out there and he'll do what he always does... get Capt. Ray B. back to wherever he is supposed to be."

"Thanks, Chris. I bet you have a lot of fun around these aeroplanes and the like, don't you?"

Chris turned and gazed off at the truck, the tents and back at me. "Well, if you enjoy sleeping outdoors all time, I suppose it's okay...until it rains...then it ain't so much fun, unless you like mud in your food, on your shoes, in your hair." Now this got us laughing again.

We both kept jabbering away as we walked back toward Snag and Charlie. Chris continued. "Like I said, I only do this in the summertime. This is my second time to go on this trip with my grandpa. The first time

92 JOSEPH A. JOHNSTON

though, he had to ride with me on the train. My folks were glad to see me too. I guess my folks let me go in hopes Grandpa will teach me a few things about life and who knows, I may even learn to fly one of them machines someday. Then again maybe they needed a little peace and quiet. Well, one good thing about it is that I will see a lot of the countryside. Now my folks like to travel too and they've taken me to a lot of places I will long remember."

I was caught up in listening to Chris tell of his travels, wishing I had to the chance to do the same, but knew from our poor means, that would be a dream for a long time to come.

"Chris, I bet that traveling is really exciting even with the mud from time to time."

More chuckling by Chris and me. Then I looked at him rather strangely, I guess, thinking over what he had just said about learning how to fly these aeroplanes. I couldn't believe anyone in their right mind would want to take a chance of flying around in the skies and then the darn contraption giving out of gas and falling out of the sky. I was thinking like Capt. Ray B. and his run of bad luck. I knew such an idea was not for this country boy for sure, at least while I was still in my right mind.

"Chris, if it's all the same to you, I wish you good luck on learning to fly, but these things are a tad too scary for me. Now I'd dearly love to come over and see them Saturday, but a couple of things ain't gonna let me."

CHRIS HAS A GOOD AND CARING HEART

Chris looked at me seriously. "Earl D., how come you can't come over and see the show at least? No one will make you ride in a plane if you don't want to you know."

I had to laugh again…"Well, Chris, first off they cost like thunder to ride in one, and second of all, I ain't hankering to ride in one no matter what. The other problem is my folks have a great fear of me even getting close to any kind of machinery, and that includes aeroplanes. 'Course I'm not sure why as I don't think they've ever been close to one either. They don't even know I'm here helping Capt. Ray B. out! And the second thing is, we aren't exactly rich. Even twenty-five cents is hard to come by these days."

Chris was nodding his head as if he understood our poor conditions as I continued with my tale. "Now Capt. Ray B. did mention a re-ward for helping him out, but even then I'm not sure my folks are going to let me come out here. I hope they do, but I know my folks are awfully skittish about this sort of thing."

CHRIS MAKES US ANOTHER GOOD DEAL

Chris had a sad look on his face. "I guess I can understand what you're saying about your folks. But you know there's no harm in just looking at the aeroplanes. Now I tell you what… if your folks will let you come, shucks you all come up to the gate and I'll get you and Snag both in for free…how about them apples? Where do you live around here, Earl D.? Is it very far from here?"

I looked at him with a smile, "That's awful nice of you to offer to help me and Snag, but Snag may be the only one to show up. Now we live just a hop and a skip from here" Then I explained where we lived, even drawing out a little map in the dirt and telling him what our place looked like an all.

94 JOSEPH A. JOHNSTON

"There you be, Mr. Chris. X marks the spot of our little bit of heaven right here in Blanchard forks. Why come you want to know all this?"

Chris broke my spell with a great sounding idea. "Well, I was thinking of a way to maybe help you out. How about in the morning, I grab one of Grandpa's horses and ride out to see you… maybe to even meet your folks. I'm a pretty good talker and I bet between you and me, we could get your folks to let you come to the air show. How about that?"

I was mumbling something when Chris suddenly took the stick from my hand then began making a drawing in the dirt. He drew a big round face in the soft dirt adding two eyes and a dot for a nose and a line to make a big smile. Then he gave me an explanation of it.

"Earl D., when everything seems to go wrong, you always have to smile and keep going no matter how hard and long the journey. That's something else my folks taught me. And one of their favorite sayings is, 'Stay positive of mind and keep a strong faith.' So I do. And if you think of this drawing whenever things aren't going right, you'll feel much better afterwards. Shoot I draw these things out all the time at school and wherever I'm at. That way folks will always know I like happy and smiling folks around me."

I stood there thinking again how smart this young feller was, knowing so much about life, and here Snag and me could hardly find the outhouse without help. Mercy.

I shook my head a little. "Chris, that's mighty nice of you to offer to come talk to my folks, but you'd prob'bly just be wasting your time. My folks are pretty hard headed on some things an' I'm 'fraid this is one of those times. But… now if'n you want to come out to the place, shoot that'd be right nice. We'd be glad to

SNAG & ME – A FLYING IN A JENNY   95

have you. Then you could see where we lived. Nothing fancy mind you, but it's home."

"I'll be there… and I bet it's a nice place too. How about I come for breakfast?"

HOW TO HANDLE THIS INVITATION TO BREAKFAST

Now this got me cold for sure. "What time you get up around here, Chris?"

He smiled. "Earl D. with all the skeeters and the snoring from my grandpa, you don't sleep late around here. Besides, Grandpa is up at daybreak every morning rain or shine getting things ready for the day and putting on a pot of coffee over the fire, or we're up and packing, heading on down the road someplace between here and there. Now I'll come if you think your folks would have me."

I looked at him again… not sure he would help me get to this show even if he did show up. I just didn't believe he could convince Mama or Papa, but we had nothing to loose so I agreed.

"Tell you what, Chris, as soon as you can, after you get up, come on. Mama'll have breakfast on the table… she rises early too and so does Papa. If you get there a tad late, she'll save you some."

Snag had heard the last part of this deal about 'something to eat' and decided he would come for breakfast too. Mercy, I could only hope Mama would make enough biscuits and Nell Faye wouldn't go plumb crazy over this. Whew, so much for one poor head like mine.

"Okay, my friend," Chris replied, "It's a deal… I'll see you in the morning bright and early."

Snag chimed in, "Yeah boy, Chris, now I can tell ya pronto like, Earl D.'s ma can cook like you wouldn't believe. I know for a fact 'cause I eat there purty much of the time."

We were all grins. "Chris, I hope you can do all this without you get'n into trouble with your grandpa, but I tell you right now, even though we just met you, we think you're a pretty straight shooter. Thank you again."

"Oh goodness, Earl D., I do that all the time when I see fellers or girls outside the fence just dying to get in and see the aeroplanes up close. My grandpa don't care, and the other folks with the show don't care either as long as I don't let too many young'uns in." He began to chuckle.

We both shook his hand and told him we would really try and get over here one way or the other, even if his visit didn't convince my folks. I knew Snag would no matter what. With that he told me I better hurry along while his grandpa was in a good mood.

Snag and I rushed back to the hitching post. Snag unhitched the reins, trying to hold onto Charlie at the same time while I struggled to get back on his bony back. Then I helped Snag up, talking at the same time.

HEADING FOR THE BOTTOMS AND CAPT. RAY B.

"Snag, boy day, we've got to hurry before it gets any later or Papa is going to have my hide for being out so late.

Snag didn't seem too concerned as he struggled to get up on Charlie's back behind me. "Why is it, Earl D., you worry so much about every little thing?"

"Well, Snag, I can't help it if my folks tell me to do something and most times I do what they tell me 'cause I don't like trouble."

Snag was interested in what all Chris and me was talking about. I had to put a damper on the questions until we had time to sit and talk a spell…not sure when that would be either.

"Never mind right now, Snag… we gotta get before Mr. Einberger changes his mind."

We were up and ready to trot. As we sat there on Charlie's back we waved so-long one more time to Chris as his grandpa retrieved a horse and climbed in the saddle, pulling the containers of gas up and tying them to the saddle horn. One of the other fellers, the one called Big Jim grabbed a leather bag full of something heavy and mounted another horse.

We waited until they were coming out the gate and then we led them off for Hansom bottoms aboard Charlie with Skip trotting off ahead. We had to keep a good trot going 'cause the horses were about to run over us as Mr. Einberger was telling us to get a move on.

As we trotted along I told Snag some of what Chris had said. Needless to say this was pleasing to both of us. We both agreed if he lived around here we'd sure be chums with him. But even if Chris came to breakfast, I knew I still faced a problem of convincing Mama and Papa.

It seemed in just a short while we had led the men back to Hansen Bottoms and Capt. Ray B.

CAPT. RAY B. AND MR. SPARKS HAVE WORDS

When we arrived, Capt. Ray B. and Mr. Sparks instantly shared some strong words, as Mr. Sparks climbed down out of the saddle and yelled, "Ray B., you crazy jackass, you must have beans for brains to

98 JOSEPH A. JOHNSTON

pull another stunt like this! I'm just sick and tired of having to do this every place we go!"

Capt. Ray B. didn't take too kindly to these words as he hollered right back. "Well, you old coot, speaking of brains, if your brains were put in a bee's tooth, it'd fly back'ards and kiss mule for a morning glory."

The first thing you know they were both in the grass 'rasseling' like a couple of bears, both cussing an' pulling hair, each trying to choke the other. Capt. Ray won out when he clamped down on Mr. Sparks' ear with his teeth causing him to yell like he'd been shot. "All right, you crazy coyote, oooooooooohhhhhhhh, turn me loose...ooooooohhhh, you win, you win...all right," he kept up the yelping.

With that last exchange of pain, Capt. Ray B. turned loose his ear. It was bleeding like a stuck hawg. Capt. Ray. B. was spitting and screaming at Mister Sparks, "You old varmint, when's the last time you took a bath? Yore ear tasted terrible!"

This got Mr. Sparks all riled up again. "Juss a galldarn minute you crazy jackass, who you calling dirty?" As Mr. Sparks seemed like he was about to flay into Capt. Ray B. again, this caused the other feller, Big Jim, who was much bigger than Capt. Ray B. or Mr. Sparks Einberger, to step in between them, laughing out loud at them both.

"You fellers ought to see yourselves...now let's quit all this silliness before you really hurt one another. This ain't no way for old friends like you two to get along. Besides the boys here will think you hate one another and that wouldn't be nice either. So, what say you both shake hands and lets get this machine running and heading for the park 'fore dark." With that he laughed some more, and we joined in too. I was glad to see them

SNAG & ME – A FLYING IN A JENNY   99

stop the feuding, though they didn't act like they wanted to shake hands, but they did.

Snag and I were still giggling at the sight of them two. They were a mess for sure. They both were covered with grass stains all over them and probably later tonight they would feel the chigger bites that got on them while rolling around in that grass.

There was Mr. Sparks with a bloody ear and looking like he was ready to leave out of here. Then not but a few feet away stood Capt. Ray B. with a bloody mouth! He was still spitting while digging around in his cockpit screaming for a rag. Finding one, he wiped his mouth again and again, yelling for something to wash his mouth out with. Big Jim, laughing even louder now offered him a swig of gasoline. This caused Mr. Sparks to holler… "Yeah, give him a big dose of it and when he fires up that stinking cigar of his, we'll see the last of him!"

Now we weren't sure what was going on here but I knew if that powerful stuff was lit off, it'd make a mess of things. I was glad when Capt. Ray B. told him thanks anyway, he' trot down to the creek and wash his mouth out. And he did, followed by Mr. Sparks, I guess to sort of wash his ear off a bit.

Shortly they were both back and I guess on friendly terms again.

We looked at Capt. Ray B. and then he grinned real big. "Fellers, if you evah tangle with an old coot like Sparks there, make sure they have clean ears 'fore you chomp down on them." This just caused us all to start laughing again…all except Mr. Einberger. He was still fussing away.

Snag turned to me with a grin and said, "I ain't seen this much fun since Grandpa stirred up a hornets nest in the outhouse!"

100   JOSEPH A. JOHNSTON

This mess of words from Snag only got us all tickled again. We even got a smile out of Mr. Sparks who was trying to place a rag on his ear to slow down the bleeding. Big Jim finally tore the rags and sort of wrapped them around his head and ears. Now he looked really strange.

GETTING THE AEROPLANE READY FOR TAKE OFF

Once Mr. Sparks was satisfied his ear wasn't going to bleed all day, he was ready to get the gas into the aeroplane. With some help from Big Jim, they both grunted loudly as they lifted the cans up over the aeroplane. Opening a cap between the two seats, they proceeded to pour the gasoline into the gas tank. At the same time they were telling Capt. Ray B. not to light up his cigar or else he'd blow us all to kingdom come!

That scared me after remembering the earlier fright when Mr. Einberger was filling them cans. Snag seeing me get scared, caused us both to run for the woods. Capt. Ray B. hollered out to us, "Hang on, fellers, don't run off just yet…I ain't gonna blow nobody up! Besides, I owe you both for your troubles."

We ambled back over near the aeroplane where he was standing with a fresh cigar dangling in his lips. He hadn't fired it up yet, so I guess we were safe. He looked at us both. "Fellers, now let me tell you… whatever you do don't ever start smoking these stinking cigars or them gosh awful cigarettes. They will cause you misery and then some. But, let's get to what I said I'd do if you helped me out … and you did, and I thank you both. Then he reached into his pocket, pulling out some large tickets.

"Here," he said. "These will get you and a couple of other folks into see our show."

I stuttered, "Mr. Capt. Ray B., we met that feller Chris you were telling us about and he said if we could get our folks to let us come to the park, he'd get us in for free."

"Well, fellers, that's all well and good on Chris's part, but just to be safe, take these tickets anyway. Shoot, you can bring your folks if you like. Again I want to thank you both for getting this old coot to come an' rescue me again." He turned and laughed at Mr. Sparks who was finishing the job of pouring in the gasoline.

Mr. Sparks and Big Jim started a slow walk around the aeroplane looking over every inch of it so it seemed. Big Jim was saying this was to make sure no parts had fallen off when Capt. Ray B. dropped down out of the sky. Just something to make sure I guess that it could still fly after plopping down in the field here.

Mr. Sparks soon hollered at Capt. Ray B. again as he and Big Jim went to the front of the aeroplane.

"Okay, you jackass, think you can find your way to the cockpit without get'n lost?"

Capt. Ray B. gritted his teeth and looked at us. "Fellers, you see what a great aviator has to put up with from time to time?" We just stood there and grinned, not sure how to reply. He reached down and shook our hands…."Okay fellers, I'll see you later—that is, if I can get this thing off the ground. If not, I'll see you in the big hanger in the sky." With that he laughed out loud as he climbed back into the aeroplane called Angel Wings.

THE AEROPLANE NAMED ANGEL WINGS COMES ALIVE

About this time Mr. Sparks yelled out again to Capt. Ray B. "Make contact, you jackass!" We didn't know

102   JOSEPH A. JOHNSTON

what in the world that meant either, but we knew that name he yelled out wasn't too friendly. We were glued to the ground trying not to miss a thing of all the goings on. We stood there watching each little move, not knowing what was going to happen next, but for sure, we knew something was going to bust loose just any second.

It was so exciting watching something happen that we had never seen before. There we stood, both shaking like leaves on a tree. Skip sensing our nerves being rattled a bit and feeling us shaking, had once again cowered between us. Even Charlie was nervous and letting out a few whennies of his own. We had him tied real good to a nearby maple tree. I was fearful that he might pull right out of his bridle and head for the barn if the commotion got too loud.

With a few more words between them, Capt. Ray B. was messing around with something and then looked like he was going to climb out of the bright, yellow flying machine. He changed his mind, I guess, as he began adjusting his helmet and the cigar between his teeth. Now they all commenced yelling back and forth again, as Mr. Sparks grabbed the propeller thing again, giving a loud grunt as he pulled the blade, which only went around a little bit. He grabbed it again and gave another hard pull and another loud grunt. Then Big Jim took a try at it; more grunting. They kept this up until both were pretty well winded.

Once again Mr. Sparks was yelling at Capt. B. "All right, world famous crash lander, you think you can find the cotton pick'n magneto switch? Now please try to find it and turn it to the place where it said ON. And, kind sir, if you don't mind too much and it won't put you out, kindly set the throttle so it will fire! If that's too tough for yore pea brain, then let's swap places and you can pull this daggum prop for while!"

SNAG & ME – A FLYING IN A JENNY   103

Capt. Ray B., who was laughing at the situation, hollered back... "Well, you old knot head, I'm way ahead of you. You sure you didn't pour water in the tank instead of gas?"

This caused some more hard looks between them. With one more loud grunt, Mr. Sparks gave the propeller a real hard pull...this time, the engine caught, and did it ever! Mercy sakes, smoke came boiling out of that engine like it was on fire! The racket it made would wake the dead! And all the dust and leaves it was blowing back at us spooked us and ole Charlie too. He was about to pull down the small tree we had him hitched to! Even Skip was hightailing back into the bushes. Snag and me hung on for dear life from the wind being whupped up by this aeroplane.

Capt. Ray B., smiling with his cigar now lit and just a smoking, waved as the aeroplane began to roll forward as he turned it to the long side of the pasture.

Snag and me were praying silently that he'd be okay in this flying contraption and make it to the park in one piece. As we watched in wonder, he did something to cause the plane to roar even louder, then it started going real fast, bouncing up and down as it hit those bumps. Down across the pasture he went, running over bushes, more bouncing up and down, then finally rising up sharply, barely missing the treetops at the end.

CAPT. RAY B. WAS ON HIS WAY

We were clapping our hands like crazy, happy that Capt. Ray B. got that flying machine into the air and on his way to the park. Soon he was above the trees, as we waved like crazy but doubted if he could see us by now. Then he disappeared, but we heard the aeroplane for quite a while. I was sure anybody outside in their gardens could

104   JOSEPH A. JOHNSTON

hear that engine noise and was probably wondering what in heavens name was flying over their heads.

"Golleeeeee, did you see that, Earl D.?" yelled Snag.

"Yep," I replied. "Now you know why I ain't gonna ever try and fly in one of them things. They're too loud; they nearly catch on fire; they fall out of the sky and if a feller's not careful, he could get killed messing with 'em!"

Snag gave me that look of disbelief then shouted back at me.

"Awwww, Earl D., that's what makes them aeroplanes that much more ex-cit'n. I was just plumb beside myself and felt so unnecessary just a look'n at all the fun Capt. Ray B. was having, a-fly'n that contraption."

"Maybe so if you like that sort of thing, Snag, but for me, you can have all my share of it. I don't want no part of anything to do with such a contraption. I know Heaven is a nice place, but no sense in rushing it and a body shorely would if'n they were to be messing with one of those fly'n machines."

We watched as Mr. Sparks and Big Jim climbed onto their horses, saying a quick thank you and telling that they hoped they would see us at the park on Saturday. Then just as quickly, they goosed their horses, turned and rode off through the pasture toward Blanchard Forks.

Snag and me stared as they rode off. Snag was thinking the same thing as me I suppose.

"Earl D., could you believe what we just heard? That old coot was about half friendly there. You reckon he's had a change of heart or something? I mean, we did them a heap of a big favor juss leadin' 'em out here. What you make of that?"

"Well, Snag, maybe their folks did teach 'em a few nice things to say when folks help you out. I believe it's only proper to say 'thank you' when a body does you a favor. No matter, what's important is, we helped Capt. Ray B. out and he gave us some tickets to see the aeroplanes. Now all we gotta do is get our folks to agreeing to let us use them."

We stared off at the other two riders as they disappeared into the woods. Snag made one more remark about these two fellows.

MORE YAKKING ABOUT A LOT OF NUTTIN'

"You know, Earl D., them two fellers had me kinda worried for a spell an' I was 'bout ready to wish a booger to get after 'em someday. Now guess I'll have to change my wish."

"Maybe so, Snag. Ya know, I think we'll have to call it a day for fishing too. It's late and we gotta scat for the house or else you know I will catch blue blazes. Guess them bream will have to wait another time ole chum 'cause the sun is settin' fast an' I have to get back or Papa will come looking for me and he won't be too happy having to do that. You know how upset he gets when I don't get Charlie back to the barn 'fore dark thirty, an' Mama has probably got supper ready too."

Snag agreed with me. "Yep, Pa's the same. He don't mind me using Lester, but I best not treat him badly or keep him out too long. If'n I do, he usually has a switch to teach me how to get the mule back home when I'm supposed to."

I had to chuckle at my pal. "Awww, Snag, you think you're gonna make me believe your pa really gets a switch after you?"

Snag was giggling, in between his tales of pain 'cause the stories were going to be getting bigger and bigger. This next spasm he actually grabbed my arm to stop me so I wouldn't lose a word he was about to say.

"Earl D., now stand still a minute an' let me tell ya the gospel truth. Pa has sent me after switches more'n once... an' ever' time he'd lay 'em on me, they'd break. Now he was doing his best mind you to wearing me out. Next thing you know, I'd have to limp outside, pain and all and fetch another one. This time bigger than the last'un so it wouldn't break... but they would. Finally when I had to haul a log in, he called it a day saying he just didn't have enough strength left to raise it against me. I was glad for the relief!"

Now this got me laughing like I had lost my mind, and he was laughing just as hard. My chum was an expert at telling tall tales... Well, maybe second to Capt Crazy Ray B. Ricker who I think was the champ at this point. Snag was forever stretching his tales way beyond belief. He knew how to get me going too. Well, I knew his folks tried to catch him a few times for doing something mischievous, but most times he'd luck out and hide until they got over their angry spell. Yep, he was one lucky rascal for sure.

With that, we hurriedly crossed the creek to gather up our fishing poles and worms, then crossing back over the log one more time, we were ready to haul for home.

Our next problem was getting Charlie to be still long enough for us to get back on his bony back so we could leave. I think he was still upset over all the noise that Capt. Ray B. made in that aeroplane. Through some more struggling, we were at last heading for home. Charlie knew it too for he was really trotting along now, causing us to bounce really bad. I knew if this lasted too long, we wouldn't be able to sit for a spell.

"Snag, how we gonna tell our folks about this?" I asked, as we bounced along.

SNAG & ME – A FLYING IN A JENNY   107

"Shucks, Earl D., juss let it roll off yore tongue natchurl like an' they'll be right proud of you for helping out a famous aviator like Capt. Ray B. Shoot-fire; show 'em the tickets he gave us! They'll prob'bly give you a extra piece of pie or something!"

He was laughing in my ear, but I knew it wasn't going to be that easy. Snag never seemed to have any trouble going here and there, or doing this or that. His folks must really like to get shed of him or else he was one smooth talker.

We rounded the corner of our pasture as I began bringing Charlie to a stop after hollering WHOA several times.

Snag quickly slid off Charlie's back with his fishing pole. I bid him and Skip goodbye, then headed Charlie for the barn with a last reminder to Snag about our early breakfast with Chris. Maybe if we didn't get to go to the park to see them aeroplanes on Saturday, we could at least try again to catch some bream or go swimming or do sometime during the day. None of that sounded good since we would be missing the excitement of a lifetime. Well, I was thinking, at least we saw an aeroplane up close and got to meet Capt. Ray B. too. Not bad for a couple of little country boys like Snag and me to have all that excitement in one setting. Not bad at all.

Another thought came to mind as I guided Charlie up the back lot to the barn. Our fishing adventures of late hadn't always panned out too well. If we did go again on Saturday, for once, it would be nice to bring home a mess of fish that Mama would feel like cooking and Nell Faye wouldn't laugh her self crazy over my catch, but that hadn't happened yet. When I did bring home a few, she'd just bust out laughing telling me they looked more like minnows than fish. I made a promise

108 JOSEPH A. JOHNSTON

to one day catch a sack full, and big'uns too just to make her eat her words. So far Mama hadn't seen any worth messing with. I promised myself that one of these days we'd catch a mess then let her see what good fishermen we really were.

PREPARING FOR THE SHOW IN THE KITCHEN

Getting ole Charlie settled in, I laid out some hay and fresh water for him as I began pondering how I was going to explain all of this exciting day to Mama so she could help me explain it to Papa. I knew it wasn't going to be an easy chore. Pacing my footsteps to the house, I ran through my mind all the many ways to try and explain this to Mama so she could explain it to Papa.

I dearly loved my papa, but it seemed at times when I tried to explain something to him, it didn't always work out like I wanted it to. He'd listen closely, but if I hit a bad spot trying to explain to him what was on my mind, he would give me such a look as to make me nervous as a cat stealing milk. My tongue would just quit working all together. Then he'd get up from where he was sitting, pat me on the back and tell me to try again later when I got it right. So much for trying to talk to Papa about anything serious—especially something as serious as aeroplanes.

His explanation for giving me the serious looks was to make sure I was always telling the truth. He was convinced if I wasn't telling the truth, I would trip over my tongue and my story would fall plumb apart. Even when I was telling the truth, which is most of the time, or even when I tried to stretch it a mite, it didn't make any difference. Often when I felt something was important to talk about, I couldn't get through a whole story with him until he would leave me standing there with my mouth ajar, or tell me to go explain it to Mama. So, I knew right from the start there was no need even trying to tell Papa about the aeroplanes. Mama was my last hope.

TELLING MAMA ABOUT CAPT. RAY B. RICKER

Supper was almost ready when I finally ambled through the kitchen door. Sitting down heavily on the bench, I rested my chin in my hands and pondered my next move. Mama stopped her kitchen work and turned to me.

"Well, howdy, Earl D., you an' Snag catch a mess of fish for supper?"

That got my attention. "Uuuh, no ma'am, Mama. We had a case of bad luck with the fish today. I hope you wasn't really waiting on me an Snag to bring a mess of fish home for supper!"

She began to laugh, "I know you two boys have a lot fun fishing, swimming and just being boys. If you catch fish that's good, but I always prepare my suppers and dinners from what I know to be a sure thing, and that's most of the time. Now I have noticed for a long time, you and Snag never seem to bring enough home to worry with. Now maybe next time you might prove me wrong. Of course, if you do, I'll fix up whatever you bring. That's after you've scaled and cleaned them up good first!"

I looked around the kitchen. "Where's Papa?"

"Your papa is on the front porch taking a much needed rest and reading the almanac. It seems that we weren't supposed to be getting the bad storms like we had last night."

110   JOSEPH A. JOHNSTON

I knew Papa believed in the Almanac just about as much as he believed in the Bible. He called it the 'Poor Farmers' Bible.' He often said our bountiful crops were because of two great things… the blessing from God and the good words from the Almanac. Made sense to me.

I gazed again at Mama. I sensed she knew something was on my mind from my strange actions. She was standing there looking at me pretty closely, then she started asking questions.

"Now, are you ready to tell me about all the bad luck you had today? By the way, what in tarnation was all that racket I heard right before you came home? Sounded like an aeroplane or something roaring right overhead but it was out of sight before we could all drop everything and run out to see."

I was starting to get nervous already. "Mama, you better sit down so I can tell you what happened this afternoon."

She got a real serious look on her face as she dried off her hands with her apron and sat down across the table staring at me.

TALES OF AEROPLANES, AVIATORS AND CHRIS COMING FOR BREAKFAST

I ran through the whole episode. She laughed every now and then as I told about me and Snag seeing this aeroplane plop down in the pasture and being scared out of our wits. She really let out a roar when I explained how Charlie and Skip reacted to all this noise of the aeroplane when it came flying in over our heads. Then how we went and met this aviator named Capt. Crazy Ray B. Ricker, and going over to the park to get him some help.

Next I told her about Snag and Mr. Sparks getting into it, and the rasseling match between Capt. Ray B. and Mr. Sparks Einberger. Finally, I told her about meeting this sharp-minded little feller named Chris.

Mama stopped me in my tracks. "Did I hear you say Mr. Sparks? Is he some kin folk of Reverend Sparks at church?"

"Oh, no ma'am, Mama, I wouldn't think so 'cause he's not from around these parts. It's really just a nickname of sorts. The new feller we met, Chris, said it had to do with something working around the aeroplanes and such. His real name is Mr. Gus Einberger and he just happens to be Chris's grandpa."

She seemed satisfied with the name Sparks, so she motioned for me to continue.

"Mama, you wouldn't believe how smart this little feller Chris is. I mean he's just right up there with the brains. And you know what else? He lives way down in a place called Tampa, Florida. Got an ocean right there close by and he goes swimming in it. He talked of big sandy beaches an' all. You know what else?"

Mama was shaking her head with a grin big as ever as I told her more about Chris. "Mama, he has a real live orange tree growing in his back yard and he can pick one right off the tree and gobble it down anytime he likes. Ain't that something? And he even says it's like summertime down there nearly all year round."

Mama was all ears as I went on and on about Chris, then I dropped a little hint about tomorrow. "Mama, I'm hoping you don't mind, but I sort of invited him for breakfast; that is, if it's okay with you."

I wasn't sure what to expect as Mama studied my last remarks about breakfast for a stranger. "

112   JOSEPH A. JOHNSTON

"Now Earl D., you know I don't mind sharing what little we have with folks and maybe this little feller Chris might just be yearning for a home cooked breakfast… so I'll say it's okay. Anyway it's too late to say 'no' since you didn't give me much wiggle room to say different."

I smiled and thanked her, then quietly told her that Snag would probably be here for breakfast too. Now this got her attention good. "Earl D. would you mind telling me if the whole county is coming for breakfast? I don't think we can feed an army of folks. I think maybe I best pack up and leave before this storm of folks hits us. Mercy, I would have to start making biscuits now!"

"No ma'am, Mama, please don't run off… it's just them two, that's all… honest injun."

She calmed down a bit. "Well, I guess it'll be all right but I know one thing for certain. Your sister, Nell Faye, won't like the idea of Snag sitting across the table staring at her that early in the morning."

"Mama, just please tell her to be nice for this time at least. Now Little Chris is a straight shooter an' I'm sure he'll find a way to make even her smile. I'm bet'n he has better table manners than Nell Faye."

"I sure hope you're right, but you know that sister of yours has a sour streak at times that would make the devil run. From the way she acts at times, a body would think we raised her on crab apples."

I laughed, "Yes'm, I know that for a fact." We both laughed.

THE STORY OF THE RASSELING MATCH

I didn't think Mama caught what I said earlier about Capt. Ray B. and Mr. Sparks getting into it with one another as I began the tale again. "Mama, you should've seen that Capt. Ray B. and Mr. Sparks having a rasseling match in that pasture. You'd have laughed yourself silly like we did."

Mama gave me serious look. "You mean to tell me that two grown men were acting childish in front of God and everybody?"

"Yes'm and it got a little heated when Capt. Ray B' bit down on Mr. Sparks' ear."

"Well, I do declare, if that don't beat all. I'm just glad it happened out in the woods and pastures so no decent folks would have to see such goings on between two grown men. Mercy, what is this world coming to? Weren't they even a little bit ashamed of how they acted?"

"Mama, they didn't hurt one another all that much and they are good friends too. And guess what else?"

"Earl D., at this point I'm afraid to ask."

I was getting excited with the thoughts of maybe something going right for once in my life as I reached into my pockets and pulled out the tickets, laying them on the table.

"Lookee Mama, these tickets are a re-ward for helping Capt. Ray B. out. Mama, surely by now you might think about letting me go to see those aeroplanes. I've got these tickets an' as a matter of fact Chris can get us in for free. Then, if you like, you, Papa, Nell Faye and even little Percy can all come to the park and see them aeroplanes too!"

MAMA PUTS A DAMPER ON MY DREAM

"Well, honey, as I said before, I'm not certain your papa will let you go and also I'm not sure he would go even with free tickets. I will just have to talk to him after supper."

114   *Joseph A. Johnston*

"Mama," I moaned, "Surely after all of this Papa might let me go to the park to see those aeroplanes. Don't you reckon?"

"Earl D., quit your moaning," she began to explain. "I'll do my best, but I can't speak for your papa, and I hate to remind you again you know how he is about those things. Especially if he thinks you might get hurt. But to be honest, I see no harm in it. Tell you what sugar. I promise that right after supper when your papa and I have our nightly talks out on the front porch, I'll try and convince him that you earned a ticket and it would be heart-breaking to deny you this once in a lifetime chance of seeing those aeroplanes."

She was now back putting the dishes on the table and with a deep sigh, told me the hard part.

"Mercy, now I'll have to prepare your papa and Nell Faye for company for breakfast too. You know, Earl D., I have a full plate and lots of it too hard swallow." She gave me a big smile, "I'll manage it somehow."

I got up and ran around the table giving her a big hug, thanking her for talking to Papa later on.

About that time I spotted Papa walking toward the barn so I quickly ran outside to help him finish up the evening chores, keeping my hopes high as we got through all that and washed up for supper.

WONDERING IF ALL MY WISHES WOULD COME TRUE TOMORROW

Later on that evening, I lay in bed hoping things would work out in my favor for once. I looked out the window into the dark, summer, night. It was warm, but thank goodness a slight breeze was moving through the open windows. I was watching the amazing fireflies

SNAG & ME – A FLYING IN A JENNY   115

zip in and out around the trees and distant meadows in the evening darkness. I just hoped we didn't have any more thunderstorms like we had last night. Once a lifetime is enough to go through one of those nearly tornado storms.

I was tossing and turning and just couldn't seem to doze off to sleep because of being in deep thoughts about all the excitement I had seen today. The bed was comfortable enough and Little Percy was on his side for a change, but there I lay… my eyes wide open.

I thought of Chris again, feeling sorry for him having to sleep on the cold ground in that tent. That must get hard on the body after a few nights and here he had been doing it for sometime. I was thinking again what a nice pal Chris would make if he lived in these parts. I could only imagine all the fun we'd have going hunting, fishing, swimming and putting up with Bubba Jean Fritzwater at school and tossing horseshoes, and maybe him telling me more about that game called *chess*.

I was thinking as smart as he seemed to be, Mrs. Thrasher would be so pleased with him. Shoot, he'd only have to go to school a half day while the rest of us dummies would struggle to make it till late afternoon, and still not know too much.

Looking outside once again I noticed the fireflies were everywhere. There must have been a million of them swooping in around the fig trees. I could hear the lonesome calls of some whippoorwills every now and then. Then I heard a dog howling in the distance. The tree frogs were so loud, I could barely hear Mama and Papa talking as they swung back and forth in the front porch swing. The swing squeaked about as loud as the frogs! I was just hoping they were discussing my trip to the park and Papa wouldn't get upset about Chris coming to breakfast.

116 JOSEPH A. JOHNSTON

After sometime, my eyes got too heavy and I drifted off to sleep with my thoughts about aeroplanes, chums, and what it would really be like to fly around in the air in one of them contraptions.

A MORNING TO REMEMBER

Morning came early as it always did, with the smell of breakfast weaving in and around the doors and floating over my bed. I didn't need an alarm clock to get up around here. If it wasn't Nell Faye trying to twist my big toe off, it would be the smells of Mama's good breakfast cooking. That always woke me up. 'Course the excitement of Chris coming to breakfast made me jump out of bed a little quicker too. In nothing flat I was into my clothes, rushing toward the back porch through the kitchen where I got my first surprise of the day. There sitting at the table already was none other than Chris… talking with Nell Faye!

He saw me and yelled out… "Good morning sleepyhead… I thought you said you got up early!"

Mama was smiling and Papa was sitting there too sipping his coffee and listening to Chris. So far no Snag, so Nell Faye still had a smile on her face. She seemed to be enjoying Chris's company. Now I liked that.

Well, I had to laugh a bit. "Morning, Chris… yeah, I'm a tad late it seems… but you can blame it on Nell Faye… she usually wakes me up with pain!"

He had a questioning look on his face. "PAIN?" he asked. I then told Nell Faye to explain it to Chris while I washed up. Off I ran to the cold well water, green soap and a quick dipping my hands it to the old basin, then onto my face. Whew, what a way to wake up.

Drying off my hands and face I noticed the horse that Chris rode over on. Nice looking too, with a nice

SNAG & ME – A FLYING IN A JENNY   *117*

looking saddle and saddlebags. Boy, would I like to have a saddle for that Charlie. Papa says he's a working mule and not a pleasure mule. That meant no saddles.

As I was about to go back inside I heard this huffing and puffing sound coming around the corner of the house. It was none other than Snag. His britches legs were all wet up to his knees from running through the early morning dew covered weeds between here and his house over on Hazard's Gap.

"Morning, Earl D.," he yelled as he quickly ran up the steps, nearly out of breath. Glancing back over his shoulder checking out the fine horse tied to the porch rail. "Mercy, that Chris rides in style, don't he?"

"Yep, he shorely does. Can you imagine me an' you with saddles for Charlie an' Lester?"

"Naaa, ain't never gonna happen, Earl D. You an me were born with hind quarters meant to ride'n them critters with just tote sacks."

He was laughing as he washed his hands before Mama would remind him to do so. Then he struggled to beat me through the kitchen door. This caused a little more laughing as we proceeded to the kitchen table next to Chris.

CHRIS IS THE CENTER OF ATTENTION FOR US ALL

Nell Faye gave her usual sour look at Snag as he was greeting Chris, but let it pass. Then she asked me if I had emptied the washbasin and rinsed it out. "Yes ma'am, my dear sister, I did for a fact, but I didn't draw you any fresh water for it." I sat down knowing she would have something to say about that.

She gave me a grin. "That's okay, brother dear, I've already washed up." Usually she got upset because I

118   JOSEPH A. JOHNSTON

wouldn't fetch her a fresh pan of water. Seems she thought I was poison or something and she didn't want to share no wash water with me, and especially Percy!

Mama was watching this whole show to make sure we didn't act like we normally did when no one was around but us. Nell Faye got just a little antsy as Snag slid down closer to the end of the table where he was directly across from her.

I was hoping this wouldn't lead to the remarks Nell Faye normally made about Snag when he dropped in for a visit… mostly at eat'n time. She'd always find something wrong with his clothes, his smell or his table manners. She was forever telling me that I needed a new friend because I was starting to act and smell just like Snag. This upset me a lot because I knew there was no way me and Snag would not be pals. I just ignored her and kept on grinning when she would get into one of her tantrums about me and Snag.

I guess Mama had already told her not to act up with Chris visiting us for breakfast. Nell Faye raised her nose anyway as she got up and began setting the plates around the table, then laying out the forks and spoons. She made sure Chris got the best looking ones; rightly so since he was company. I don't think we had two of a kind of anything. Even our plates were all different. Didn't matter, the important thing was that they did what they were supposed to do…hold food!

My sister was too particular about most things, especially when we were eating. She was always gnawing that old bone about table manners and why Percy and me made such a mess when we ate. I always thought she just liked to complain a lot. I felt that she would probably never marry anybody 'cause they would have to be really double-dumb to put up with

SNAG & ME – A FLYING IN A JENNY   119

her picky ways! Yep, I was convinced she was going to be an old maid all her life.

As I sat down at the table, I looked at Mama, but she carried on like nothing was more important at the moment than cooking breakfast and being friendly toward Chris. He was the center of attention. Papa would ask him a question or two, then Nell Faye and then Mama. One question right after the other.

Chris was enjoying this for sure as he would really use a lot of big words to explain about his folks, his dog, his games, his school chums and what life was like down in Tampa, Florida. Then telling us how exciting it was being with his sometimes grumpy grandpa on this aeroplane road show. He also mentioned he had some wonderful grandma's, grandpa's, uncles and aunts that treated him extra kind. Well, we had kinfolk too but didn't see them too often.

Somehow, Nell Faye had found a world map, one with the United States on it. She had Chris pointing out the place where he lived in Florida. Sure enough as we all crowded in to see, there was Tampa, Florida right near the ocean. Chris said it was the Gulf of Mexico. Shoot, I thought it was the ocean. Now that took some explaining to a couple of loggerheads like Snag and me.

Looking at Mama while she was busy around the kitchen I still didn't see a hint if she had anything to tell me. So far there wasn't a whisper or a special smile to let me know everything was okay on me going to the park with Snag and Chris. I was really getting nervous, wondering if she was going to tell me anything, but soon gave up as Papa tapped on his coffee cup, letting us know it was time for breakfast, but first a few words of thanks to the Good Lord.

NO WORDS FROM MAMA ABOUT MY TRIP TO THE PARK

During breakfast I would glance over at Mama every now and then trying to see if she was going to say anything about my hopeful trip to the park. But still there were no signs. Nothing. I was getting worried. Here sat Chris, she had my tickets and surely she must have talked to Papa last night. But woe was me... not one peep from her.

Chris was really enjoying his breakfast and was having a bit of a race with Snag to see who could eat the fastest. In between taking a big bite, he was thanking Mama for such a great breakfast. He was hungry that was certain, but even so, he still had good table manners. That Nell Faye was watching him and Snag like a hawk, but smiling at the same time.

The chatter continued among Papa, Mama, and Nell Faye as they were pestering Chris to death asking more questions about where he came from and what he did for fun, what his folks thought about him being so far from home. On and on it went while Snag and me just sat there, not saying too much but managing a word or two with Chris. Then Percy started mumbling something about ghosts under his bed, which caused us all to giggle a bit. But I was sure that to Percy those ghosts were real!

Just when I was beginning to think Mama had forgotten all about it, she suddenly looked right at me and winked and smiled! I know my mouth hung open, but I managed a big smile back and let it go as our secret. Then Chris spoke up at the same time.

"Mr. And Mrs. McHenry, I am just really happy to have been able to meet you all and thanks again ever so much for a wonderful breakfast. I haven't had one like this in a while. Grandpa doesn't spend a lot of time making breakfast. So, all this great food will be long remembered for sure. My folks always worry about me eat'n proper and they reminded Grandpa before we left home to make sure I eat good. They think I need to grow a little faster. I'm doing all I can do, but I stay about the same."

Mama blushed a bit as she had a few kind words for Chris. "Son, I'm so happy you came and I'm really tickled that you enjoyed my attempts at making a decent breakfast. Thank you and you can come back anytime." This of course made our new friend smile nicely too.

PAPA MAKES A SURPRISE ANNOUNCEMENT

Papa then spoke up. "Chris, we thank you too for coming by so early to have breakfast with us. I enjoyed hearing all about your travels and what all you do with your Grandpa. That really has to be an interesting line of work messing with those flying machines. I can understand why your folks would want you to go with your grandpa. Most grandpas don't have time for grandsons. So, I'd have to say you have a humdinger of a grandpa if he's willing to let you tag along with him across this big country and learn his tricks of the trade. He sounds like a feller I'd really enjoy meeting. You know, we may just surprise you tomorrow evening and come out to see what them flying machines are all about."

Chris smiled nicely at Papa. "That'd be really a nice treat for you all come out to see the aeroplanes and meet my grandpa—that is if he isn't too busy working on those contraptions. We'll be looking for you all for sure. I hope Early D. and Snag can come a little early

122 Joseph A. Johnston

too so I can show them around a bit and tell them about what we do in these road shows."

Now what Papa had said liked to have knocked me off the bench. I couldn't believe I heard Papa saying he would be going to the park, and mostly to see those aeroplanes. Miracles do happen and here was one happening right before my eyes. Whoopee!

Chris let us know that he was free to hang around us all day if we didn't mind. Snag and me both jumped up and hollered YAHOOO. Now if Papa didn't mind, we could have a lot of fun and do all we could in one day. Papa smiled and said I had the day off! Boy, this was truly starting off as a perfect day.

The only thing Papa seemed upset about was the free tickets that Capt. Ray B. had given us. He gave me a small lecture about taking things from strangers when you give them a hand of help. One rule was that you don't except any gifts, money or otherwise when you help folks in need. But seeing that this was not a normal everyday thing that happens around here, he let it be. Thank goodness.

Chris helped me out by explaining that tickets were given out a lot of times to folks who did little favors to help them set up and other chores when they would stop at these little towns.

WE MAKE IT A DAY WITH CHRIS AND LEARN A LOT

Snag ran home to tell his folks what was going on and hopefully get permission like me to have the day off. In no time flat he came running back, nearly out of breath again, hollering that his folks let him off too.

Now it looked like poor Mama would have to fix dinner for two more mouths. Snag was happy that he had managed to get the day off too and didn't have to sneak off like he normally did.

It was time to think up something to show Chris about our little world. We could take him down to the creek and show him our swimming hole and where we go fishing. Then maybe a game of horseshoes and some slingshot practice. I was betting he would enjoy this day for a long time. It would be nice to show a little city boy a thing or two about how country boys live and have fun... that is, when they weren't working.

We sat there on the back door steps trying to figure out what first to do. Then I asked, "Chris, what would you like to do?"

He just grinned and replied, "Well, fellows, whatever you normally do when you have time off to have fun. Whatever you say will be just fine with me. I'm easy to please."

This got us giggling a bit.

Snag grinned at me as he said, "I guess yore folks gonna let you go to the park tomorrow after all, old friend."

Chris was watching all this as I stood up tall, grabbing my overall straps, then proudly announced, "Yes sir, Mr. Snag, Mama convinced Papa that it was okay for me to go with you to the park! But I think mostly because Chris, the world's best friend to everybody, came to my rescue and helped me get permission."

With that, we both jumped up and down and carried on kind of silly like. Skip, who was laying out on the back porch, heard all this commotion, got excited too as he jumped up and down, barking and running around in a circle like he was chasing his own tail. This caused us all to holler.

124 JOSEPH A. JOHNSTON

Snag stopped and with a lot of gulping for some fresh air after all that excitement, blurted out, "All right, Earl D., we gotta show Chris all about our swim'n hole an' how to use a slingshot an' all—maybe some horseshoe chunking too."

Chris was sitting there taking all this in and grinning like he was really enjoying us carrying on like a couple of monkeys.

Next, we took off toward the barn and I showed Chris where Charlie slept and where the cows stood while we milked them. Then we introduced him to the world's shyest cats, Mr. Smoky and Miss Midnight. Chris scampered right up the ladder and would you believe, he was able to get close enough to pet them both. Now that was something even I had a hard time doing, and Snag had never been able to get close enough to pet them. Chris said that he just had a way with animals. Since he had heard us talking about milking cows, he did admit that milking a cow was one thing he had never tried.

I promised if we had time later on and one of our cows wandered up close enough, I would show him how to milk a cow. He got a kick out of that as he muttered, "Boy, wait till my mom and dad hear about this! They won't believe it." We all joined him, laughing crazy like.

CHRIS BRINGS IN HIS BACKPACK

We all went to the well to fetch a drink of fresh water. Chris wanted to draw the water so we let him have a go at it. He huffed and puffed and got the bucket up and back in just a shake. We all enjoyed that dipper of fresh water.

SNAG & ME – A FLYING IN A JENNY 125

Chris excused himself for a minute and ran down the steps and over to the saddlebags on his horse. In just a shake he was back with this pack, telling us he needed a table to show us something. So we headed back into the kitchen as he laid this pack on the table. Then he quickly opened up the flaps with a rush, smiling all the while.

As he opened it, Snag and me were right there looking, and even Nell Faye was leaning way over the table trying to see what was going on. Next thing we know, out comes this pretty checkerboard. We were all gawking and carrying on how pretty it was. It was made of some kind of fancy wood. Chris said it was constructed in a pattern called *inlaid wood*. All I know it was real fancy looking. It had a small drawer on each side as well. Now Mama and Papa were peering at this fancy checkerboard too. Little Percy had his chin just about in the bag. Then Chris got our attention.

"Earl D., you recall yesterday when we were talking about playing checkers and I mentioned the game of chess?"

I nodded and replied at the same time, "Yep, I sure do, an' I also remember you telling me it was a tough old game and not one for sissies."

Now Chris was laughing. "Well, I'm not saying you have to be a brave soldier, or even a high-learned person to play this game of chess. Anyone can play this fascinating game with just a little practice. Since you said you all had never heard of this game, what I want to show you is some of the basic moves, in case you ever decide to play chess. Like I said, if you could learn this game I bet you and Snag would be the talk of the town in nothing flat—especially if no one around here knows how to play it very well. Now, that is, if y'all are interested."

126 JOSEPH A. JOHNSTON

We all shouted that we were interested, including Papa and Mama and even Nell Faye. Percy was just hollering... ME TOO... ME TOO!

Chris slowly opened the little drawer of the fancy checkerboard, then started taking out these toy looking things. Some were people looking and some were...just things, is all I knew to call them at the moment. Then Chris set all these pieces on the board. One set was silver looking and the other was sort of gold looking. Chris said these were opposing kingdoms. I guessed that meant they battled somehow. I guessed right for a change.

Then Chris picked up one of the smaller ones and called it a *pawn* telling us these were the *foot soldiers* in the game of chess. Next he grabbed one with a horse and rider, which he called a *knight*, then another fancy figure he called a *bishop*. Next he picked up this larger figure that he called the *queen,* which he said was the boss of the board when things really got tough. Then he pointed out the *king,* and the castle looking things called *rooks.*

Things really got crazy as he tried to show us and explain the many moves these figures could and could not make. My head was hurting already and that Snag was cross-eyed from a brain ache.

We must have spent a whole hour trying to learn which way these things moved on that board. Even Papa was struggling trying to remember which one moved where as he asked for some paper and a pencil so he could write down which one did what to which.

Chris was really having fun teaching this old country family how to play the fancy game of chess. It was plain to see, we weren't going to learn this game in one sitting.

I noticed Chris was tiring of this and thought we best do something else. Thank goodness Papa saw it

SNAG & ME – A FLYING IN A JENNY   127

too, telling us we needed to take a break from this for a spell. "Earl D., how about you, Chris and Snag taking a rest from all this and go outside for a bit. You need to show Chris a few things about our place, something that would be of interest to him and he might remember some day down the road."

WE GOT SOME LESSONS FROM A FELLOW NAMED CHRIS

We were out the door in a flash, leaving the game of chess for our folks to worry with. Snag and I had our slingshots already and had gathered up some small rocks to practice shooting at some tin cans on the fence post. Chris followed us and seemed happy to be doing something else. He also thought it might be fun to live on a farm.

"Chris, it might look like fun to you right now, but I gotta tell ya, it ain't!" Snag said. "If'n ya had to get up ever' morning an' start a fire for a cranky ole wood stove 'fore daybreak, then go milk the stubborn old cows, slop the hawgs, feed the chickens, mess around in the garden an' all them other chores, I think you'd be much happier staying down there where ya can go out into the ocean."

Chris looked at Snag in a funny way. "Oh yeah, I know, Snag. Living on a farm is work and lots of it. But you know, that's what gives a person pride in seeing what happens when he works hard at whatever he's doing. Now I can see from looking around here that Earl D. and his folks have to work pretty hard to keep this big place looking good all the time, and I imagine you and your folks do too. I'm just saying that I really admire folks who work hard and enjoy their work.

128 JOSEPH A. JOHNSTON

That's why this place and others I've seen from the road around here look so nice."

I hollered, "AMEN to that, Chris. I work pretty hard around here, especially in the summertime."

Snag let us know he worked hard too, saying, "Shoot, my middle name is work!" We all giggled at that remark.

GETTING WHUPPED AT SLINGSHOT SHOOTOUT

Now we were getting all ready to teach Chris a thing or two about slingshots and the art of knocking over tin cans with them. We set the cans on the fence posts then stepped off a few paces, getting out our trusted homemade slingshots and preparing for a shoot off. I was hoping we'd be able to teach Chris a couple of things about how good we were at slingshots and knocking over tin cans. But instead we fizzled out like a flickering candlelight in a rainstorm.

Snag, wanting to be first in showing his stuff at this sort of thing, proceeded to educate Chris on the fine art of holding the slingshot. Next he showed him how to place a small rock in the pouch, then how to draw it back carefully, making a bead on whatever it is you are trying to hit—in this case, a tin can. Chris was paying real close attention as Snag kept yakking. At last he began to draw the sling back as far as the old rubber bands would let him, then he let the rock fly... ZING. He missed the can.

After three shots with no hits, Snag told me to take a turn at it. My slingshot was about the same as Snag's. We had made them about the same time. I knew I wasn't very good at this either, but felt in the interest of teaching Chris a little something about what we country boys did for fun, I would try my luck at it. After the third try, I finally hit the can and knocked it off.

This got Snag going, "Earl D., you fudged on the line… now back up and do that last shot again."

I went and set the can back up on the post… then stood where Snag said I was supposed to. I drew a bead on that old rusty can… Zing…. Missed it a mile!

About this time Chris was asking to try shooting at the cans, telling us he felt like he had a grip on what we were trying to do. So, we let him have one of the slingshots. He took one of the rocks, loaded it in the pouch, and with a steady pull he managed to pull the bands real tight… he turned it loose…. Zing…bang…clang… he knocked the can off first try!

Snag was quick to remind him that it was just a lucky shot for a city boy. "Okay, Chris, let's see if you can do that again."

Chris was smiling real big now as he told us, "Fellers, you know I think I like this slingshot thing. Are they hard to make?"

We nodded our heads NO, and we watched closely as he again pulled the pouch back and let another rock fly, then another, then another, each time knocking the cans off the fence post. Now we were wondering why this Chris fellow was so stinking lucky at this slingshot shoot-out? I could've sworn he was grinning like he was pulling a fast one on us. We soon got our answer.

Chris was now about ready to roll on the ground because he was laughing so hard. We stood there looking at him as he explained, "Fellers, I didn't mean to pull a fast one on you, but I gotta confess a thing or two. You see I know a little bit about slingshots. I've made a few too with the help of my favorite Uncle Brian and my dad. They taught me how to shoot cans and targets when I was about seven years old. I just like the

130 JOSEPH A. JOHNSTON

challenge of something new and when I do, I go after it whole-hog sort of like until I get real good at it. So, don't feel bad that I beat you at shooting this thing. It's just something I got a little more practice at than maybe you fellers had. But I'll give you some hints on how to do better; that is if you are interested."

LEARNING SOME LESSONS FROM CHRIS

Snag and me felt a little put out that we had gotten beat by Chris, a city boy no less, but Chris patted us on the back telling us not to feel bad about it because he would teach us how to shoot better. With that he ran to his horse and took something else out of his saddlebag, then came running back.

What he held in his hands made out eyes pop out. A fancy slingshot like we had never seen before.

"Now fellows, this slingshot is special made. Like I said, I had some help from a super uncle and my dad. This is a rare wood that comes from Central America and it's heavy and hard as iron—nearly."

He was giggling as he let us hold it a second and sure enough, it was heavy. It had a sort of round grip on it rather than the flat things we had. Chris said it was like a pistol stock shape, which made it easier to hold and to make sure you hit what you were aiming at. Also we noticed that the wood had a face carved out in it sort of like the one he had drawn in the dirt down at the park. Chris called that his 'Mr. Smiley' and said it was a reminder to always be happy no matter what. Now that made sense to me.

Looking at this fancy slingshot I knew it had to be one of a kind for sure. The wood was a dark reddish color, nothing like we had ever seen around these parts for sure. Then he told us about the rubber bands. They

were red in color, and were made from bicycle inner tubes, which he explained were the best kind to use. Shoot, we didn't know of anyone around here that had a bicycle, so that left us out for sure.

Next he showed us the pouch, which was fancy looking too. It was made of a soft kind of leather. He said it was made at a shoe repair shop by another close friend of the family. Mercy, he had lots of good friends to help with all this stuff. All I had was Snag...and all he had was me. Not a winning pair all the time that was for sure.

We were numb-struck from what all he was telling us about his slingshot. All the wood we had around here was oak, maple, hickory, pine, cedar and a few other trees about. Our slingshot handles were made from cedar slabs that we got from the lumber mill, which we thought looked pretty good until we saw Chris's.

He kept smiling at us, talking all the while as again he took up some of the rocks and, faster than lightening, shot one shot right after another, knocking down more than one can at a time. He was good no doubt. Well, so much for showing Chris how to use a slingshot.

After this bad case of a mis-match of shooting, Chris was telling us all the while about how to hold the handle, then how to pull steady like and the release. Surprisingly, after a bit we were hitting the can more often too, though still not as good as Chris. We noticed, while shooting his slingshot, how easy it was to draw the pouch way back and then let it fly. Wow, it was some kinda super slingshot to be sure. We had to remember how it was made and try our luck at making one like his. All we needed was some bicycle inner tubes and some fancy wood from wherever he said. Mmmmm, don't reckon that is going to happen anytime soon.

The rest of the day Chris managed to beat us at horseshoes, marbles, knife throwing and even arm wrestling. That's when we decided we had been whupped enough by this little city boy who was making us country boys look pretty bad. I was thinking it was time we took him to the fishing hole. At least we beat him there. I managed to hook three little sun perch and Snag got two and Chris didn't catch a one as he laughed at his bad luck. "Well, fellow, you can't win them all, can you?"

HEADING BACK TO MORE GOOD TIMES AT THE TABLE

We all joined in laughing and having a good time as we stopped by our swimming hole and showed him our swing. Then we headed back home, stopping long enough to pick several hands full of big juicy blackberries. That Chris loved them blackberries. I told him that Mama makes blackberry pies all the time when we pick them fresh like this.

We made a hard dash for home and just as we rounded the corner of the barn, Nell Faye was ringing the dinner bell for all it was worth and hollering for us too.

We had more fun at the dinner table and what a great dinner it was. Chris again thanked Mama and Papa for the invite. We admitted too that Chris had beat the tar out of us with everything we tried to do, except fishing. This caused Nell Faye to really hee-haw.

SNAG & ME – A FLYING IN A JENNY   133

Chris was quick to make us feel better. "Awww, really now, I was just a little lucky today. Who knows, tomorrow you both could beat me at chess even."

We all laughed, knowing that would never happen.

A FUN AFTERNOON UNTIL CHIRS HAS TO SAY SO LONG

We spent the afternoon showing him the garden, letting him take a hand at picking beans and then gobbling down a whole fresh tomato. Next we went back to the barn for another look at all the animals, including Charlie, who let Chris scratch his head. Now even I had a hard time doing that. I guess Charlie was treating him nicely since he was company. Snag was watching all this as he uttered his thoughts. "Tell me, Chris, is there anything you ain't good at? Here ya are talkin' to this old hardheaded mule and he's looking like he's understanding ever'thing you say!"

Chris giggled a bit as he told us about his girlfriend, Allie. "Well, fellows, I have this friend, and her name is Allie. She has a little pony. Now I didn't use to like ponies, but she taught me not to be afraid of them. At times I wanted one and other times I didn't. Mainly because I knew we would have to keep it way out in the country some place and then I wouldn't be able to ride him often. So, whenever I managed to visit Allie, we'd ride her pony."

"Chris, ya mean yer a court'n this here gurl Allie already?" Snag asked. "Ain't ya a tad wet behind the ears to be get'n all fired serious with a gurl?"

Chris just grinned as he came out with talk sounding more like an older person than he was. "Well, I tell you, Snag, she's a special friend and we've been through a lot together. This friend just happens to be a girl. If we

134   JOSEPH A. JOHNSTON

were much older, I'm sure we'd be real serious with each other. Someday that just may happen, 'cause I think a lot of her."

That sort of put the stop to Snag's questions but I had to add my two cents worth.

"Chris, don't let that Snag fool you. He's got a girlfriend too, and her name is Bubba Jean Fritzwater!"

Now this got Snag a hollering for sure. "Don't ya believe him, Chris! He's fibbin' like a coon stealin' corn. T'ain't no way me an' that heifer'd ever be sweet on each other."

"Chris, you ought to hear Snag sweet-talk that Bubba Jean when he's a wantin' a chaw of 'baccer!"

Chris looked puzzled. "Baccer? What's that?"

"Well," I began, "it's a kind of stuff ya chew and it smells bad and looks worse. To me, it's about the same as gnawing on a dry cow pie."

Now we really had Chris going. "Cow pie?" Now you fellows are really confusing me."

With that, Snag grabbed his arm, as we were laughing and leading him outside to the barnyard. We soon spotted our goal and Snag stopped, pointed at the ground and said, "Chris, that there's a dried cow pie."

I thought Chris would bust a gut. "Snag, you mean to tell me you chew that stuff?"

Now we were all laughing as Snag hollered in defense. "Nooooo, ain't no way! What I chew once in a while is made from 'baccer plants an' somehow folks make it into what we call plugs, an' once in a while when I run short, which is most of the time, I sorta talk Bubba Jean out of a chaw. That's one itty bitty bite, mind ya."

"Chris, whatever you do, don't ever chew that stuff," I warned. "It looks terrible and smells even more terrible. I tried it only once on a dare and got sick as a buzzard. Besides, your folks would really be upset if you walked into the house looking like you just chewed on a cow pie!"

We were all giggling again as we thought it was time to teach Chris how to milk a cow... that is if he wasn't pulling our leg again.

We managed to get ole Lulu Belle, our oldest and gentlest cow, into a stall. Then we proceeded to teach Chris how to milk a cow. It was one funny time for sure. We were all laughing as Chris would give a yank and Lulu Belle would swat him with her tail. After several tries, he managed to get a little milk into a pail. He stood up and announced that he had had enough of milking for one setting.

Next we thought about something else exciting to do... and that was to meet Snag's folks. We took a quick run through the pasture over to Snag's place.

Snag's brothers and sisters and all the other dogs under the porch swarmed him as they were asking a thousand questions and liking the way he told tales. The dogs were all wanting their share of head scratching as he would go from one to the other. He had never seen so many kids and dogs in one setting it seemed. He was laughing up a storm and we were all laughing with him. We had a great time together. I knew I would remember this for a long time and I just hoped Chris would too.

We got back to my house just in time for a fresh piece of peach pie. Now we all liked that idea, especially Chris. When the table was cleared, Papa asked Chris to show them one more time about how to play that game of chess. It was fun, with all of us trying to grasp the moves and what *Check-Mate* meant and all that. Papa was really interested saying that we might order one of these games for Christmas. "You know, that'd

136 JOSEPH A. JOHNSTON

be a great game for the whole family to enjoy durin' those cold winter months when there ain't much to do around the place."

Now that was exciting news and I was looking forward to getting one of our own. That would be a fun game for sure, and mostly I wanted to be able to beat Nell Faye at it. Only time would tell.

CHRIS HEADS BACK TO THE PARK

As we all three sat on the back door steps talking up a storm about every little thing, Chris suddenly announced that he had to get on back to the park and see what he needed to do to help his grandpa for tomorrow. He told us that they would be very busy getting the aeroplanes all washed up and shiny. His grandpa and Big Jim would make sure the engines were running right and everything was working okay before tomorrow's big show. That way all the folks who wanted to ride in one could do so safely.

Mama, hearing Chris saying he had to leave pretty quickly, came out on the porch.

"Chris," she began, "I've made a blackberry pie and I want you to take it and share it with your grandpa and your other friends. We'll gather the pan back sometime tomorrow when we see you."

Now this brought on a smile for sure. "Oh, thank you kindly, Ms. McHenry. I know Grandpa would be ever so happy to have a piece of homemade pie. It's been a spell since we've had a good piece of pie. Thank you, thank you. I'll take care of your pie pan for sure."

Mama smiled and brought forth a piece of paper and pencil and asked Chris to write down his name, route and box number for Tampa, Florida so we might be able to write him after he got back home. This brought a big smile to Chris's face as he came out with a giggle…"You mean you all would really write to me?" We all nodded our heads that we would.

Chris scribbled out his name and such and at the end he drew another one of his little round faces and below it wrote… God Bless you all.

Mama was taken with that as she grabbed him up and hugged him real tight. There was a tear in her eye too as Chris smiled up at her… "Missus McHenry, I have to tell you, you are one sweet lady, just like my Mom. Thank you all for being so nice to me. I won't be forgetting this adventure anytime soon, for sure!"

We all patted him on the back as he headed to his horse. Nell Faye untied the reins from the porch and gave them to Chris. Mama waited until Chris was on the horse and sitting steady, then she handed the pie up to him. The pie was wrapped in a flour sack to keep it fresh until he got to the park.

"Now, Chris honey, do you think you can ride with just one hand okay?"

"Oh, yes ma'am, I do it a lot and I won't make him trot. We'll just go slow and easy back to the park. I sure hope we see all of you tomorrow… oh, Earl D., you and Snag try and get there a little early if you can and I'll show you what I can about what goes on in a flying show."

I looked at Mama for approval, and she nodded her head. Snag of course hollered out, "Chris, we'll be there early for sure."

We were all giggling as Chris prodded his horse and slowly headed down the lane. We all waved and hollered, "BYE, CHRIS, SEE YOU TOMORROW!" He was nodding his head okay. Mama made a final remark. "Now children, I hope you paid attention to Little Chris… for there goes a perfect little gentleman if ever I

138   *JOSEPH A. JOHNSTON*

have seen one, and he's smart as a whip too. Mercy, how proud his folks must be of him."

I felt sad and sort of hurt from Mama's little speech. She quickly sensed my hurt, and just as quick reminded us that we were still perfect in her eyes and that she loved us for being just us, but Chris was also special.

Now we had a new friend, but sadly it would only be for a few more hours. We'd have to make every minute count.

SOME SURPRISES AFTER SUPPER

After what seemed like forever, supper was finally over and everyone was getting cleaned up for bed. Mama had heated some water so I could take my tub bath out on the back porch. For once I got to take a bath before Percy! Testing the water, I pulled one more bucket from the well and mixed it in so to cool it down a bit. Shucking my clothes, I climbed in and commenced to lather up with the green-pine soap.

As I was beginning to enjoy my bath, whistling a care-free tune about nothing, listening to the evening birds, that Nell Faye snuck up behind me and silently picked up the remaining bucket of cold well water, dashing it over my head and back. Letting out a yelp, I jumped up, causing the tub to turn over with me in it, all of it, the tub, water and me falling off the back porch out into the grass.

Nell Faye yelled down at me in the dark evening light, "Next time you don't pour up clean water in the wash pan, you gonna get it worse, Mister Earl D." With that she stomped off the porch and back into the house.

Mama and Papa came running around from the front of the house after hearing all of the commotion, finding me standing there in my birthday suit, soapy,

SNAG & ME – A FLYING IN A JENNY 139

sore and mad at Nell Faye. Seeing my predicament, they asked what had happened.

My teeth were chattering like crazy as I tried to explain it all, but it only got Papa to laughing and Mama giggled a bit too. I was beginning to feel like a stepson rather than a son!

Mama, sensing my hurt feeling and pride, got Papa to draw some more water. He then poured the cold water all over me as I shook like a hound dog with an advanced case of worms! He tossed me a drying cloth as I managed to scramble back up on the steps, not knowing if I had any broken bones or not! Pulling on my clothes, I walked into the kitchen bruised and in great pain.

Nell Faye was sitting at the table making like she was reading a book under the glow of the kitchen kerosene table lamp. I saw her grin as I walked by. "I'll get you back, Nell Faye—one of these days, as sure as skunks stink!" I yelled, as I glared at her and then walked on into the back room.

Putting on my nightshirt, I climbed into bed. I was pretty upset. I wasn't sure how, if ever, to get even with a big sister who could rassel 'bout as good as any boy and could sock you in the eye in a minute. She knew I wasn't going to try anything like that, but I would think of something.

TRYING TO GO TO SLEEP WITH THOUGHTS OF TOMORROW

Nighttime in the country was pleasant if you could get your mind off of your hurt. There were so many noises to put you to sleep and to wake you up. The fireflies were out in great numbers again. Looking out the window toward the distant darkened mountains, the stars seemed to jump right out at you. I could hear the evening nightingales with their songs and the frogs croaking in the distance.

Sleep finally came as I soon forgot about Nell Faye's trick. The comfort in knowing about the coming adventure of tomorrow clouded my mind, filling it with pleasant thoughts of fun at Spaulding Park! I said my nightly prayers, with a special one for Chris that he was sleeping good and comfortable too. Then I was off to dream land.

Breakfast was fast and furious. Mama had to make me slow down with a reminder. "Earl D. you're gulping your food like the devil was trying to take it away from you! Now slow down so the angels can run him off and you can receive your food properly." Not sure what all that meant, but for sure it meant to slow down my nearly choking on each bite that I took.

The excitement about going to the park was having a great effect on me and everyone else. Nell Faye gave me her usual look and comment, "Earl D., you are positively a pig!"

Before we could get into a fracas of words, Papa was motioning for me to head out for the early morning chores. In his eyes, chores were first and fun was second.

AT LAST I AM HEADING FOR THE PARK AND FUN

Finally the magic hour arrived. I washed up quickly, and then Mama checked me over to make sure I didn't miss too many spots. She then combed my hair neatly. Then she rushed me as I changed clothes, insuring my overalls were neatly pressed. She stood back making one last check. "All right, young feller, you're

SNAG & ME – A FLYING IN A JENNY   *141*

ready. Now you go on to the park and have a good time. Now one last reminder; be extra careful and don't cause no mischief. Most importantly, don't you let Snag talk you into any devilment! If we get through with everything around here, maybe we'll see you after awhile. More than likely late this afternoon as Papa has a few more things he wants to get done before we try and head to the park."

I was nodding my head yes'm to all of the rules she always gave out and an extra nod about not letting Snag get us into any trouble. I left and noticed the tickets were on the table. I was in hopes that maybe Papa and Mama wouldn't change their mind about coming down and seeing the aeroplanes up close.

With that last gesture, I was out the front door, running down the lane toward Spaulding Park and a sight of a lifetime!

METTING SNAG AND CHRIS AT THE PARK

I had to be careful on the road, because an occasional automobile would come rumbling along. Then there would be a buggy or two, then a wagonload of folks. No one stopped and asked me if I wanted a ride. So much for being neighborly.

This was a rare thing for I seldom met anything on the road going to or from the store or school. It seemed like a lot of other folks had heard about these aeroplanes too.

As I neared the park I never saw the like of buggies, wagons and automobiles. That meant my thoughts were correct. Mercy, what a mess of folks I saw mingling around all over the place. I was hoping I could find Snag or Chris pretty quickly, but with all these folks, I might not. But my worry was short lived.

142 JOSEPH A. JOHNSTON

As I got to the main entrance to the park, there stood Snag and Chris at the front gate. Snag was already arguing about taking Skip in to see the aeroplanes too! I walked up and was about ready to ignore the discussion between Snag and one of the ticket takers, Mr. Abercromby, a middle aged man, who owned the only grist mill in the county. Snag spotted me and waved me over to help him declare that Skip was smarter than most humans and wouldn't cause a ruckus or try and fly off in one of them aeroplanes.

Mr. Abercromby wasn't giving an inch. Chris was trying to get permission too. Snag was really getting upset and I didn't want him to get us both run off before we ever got in!

A little luck came our way. We spotted Capt. Ray B. coming up to the gate. With him and Chris both arguing about letting Skip in, it was finally agreed, but only if Skip was on a rope that would prevent him from running around all over the place.

This quick plea on their part did the trick. Capt. Ray B. got us some rope from someplace and we were in at last! Poor Skip wasn't used to being tied to anything and didn't like this new rope around his neck one little bit. It was a chore just trying to get him to move.

THE PARK WAS FULL OF FOLKS AND GOING'S ON

The park was crowded. There were lots of folks selling everything from soup to hay it seemed. There were more automobiles inside the park as well. Folks from all over the county I suppose had heard about these aeroplanes and like us, just had to see them up close. 'Course, we were one step in front of them since we had already gotten a close look and meeting a world famous aviator to boot.

SNAG & ME – A FLYING IN A JENNY   143

This was like a circus! The air was filled with some mouth- watering aromas too. The folks from Gospel Corner Baptist were selling home made slices of pie and lemonade, while the 4H club from Moutainberg was selling smoked and grilled meat with homemade bread. There was lots of singing going on too. Even the Sweeny family was there singing hymns for everyone. There was one feller playing a harmonica, which got our attention. That was one thing we forgot to show Chris… with our luck, he would probably be playing it as good as Mr. Henry!

Folks were tossing horseshoes, girls were showing off the dresses their ma's had made, and boys were standing around bragging about everything. There were quilts for sell, along with jars of fruit and beans, hams and the like. Folks were picking guitars and fiddle playing too. Some people were ringing pretty bells, making some heavenly music that everyone was enjoying. They were from Bowieville, the same group that played at our church this past Christmas. But the main show was the aeroplanes and everyone was flocking around them.

FOLKS TAKING A RIDE INTO THE SKY

As we were wandering down near the aeorplanes, folks had already lined up, paying their three dollars to go for a ride in one of the aeroplanes. I was wondering where in the world they got the three dollars! Guess some folks were much better off than others. I quickly noticed that there were three aeroplanes instead of two. One had showed up that I guess Chris hadn't known about. They all had brightly colored wings, mostly yellow and red, and one had blue and white strips.

144 JOSEPH A. JOHNSTON

We watched excitedly as Capt. Ray B. was loading a scared little man in his plane for a ride. The little man would get in and then he would crawl back out right before Capt. Ray B. and Mr. Sparks could get the engine started. They offered him his money back but he would only shake his head 'no' and jump back in the seat as if he was ready to ride. Again he looked like he was going to climb out, as Mr. Sparks' was getting ready to pull on the propeller. This seemed to get Mr. Sparks dander up a tad, looking as though he had had enough of this foolishness. He threw his cap down and walked around to the little man who was about ready to climb out again. He said something to him, which we couldn't hear, but the man must have thought best to stay put as he ducked down inside the seat and never raised his head again.

They finally got the engine started as Capt. Ray B. waved at everyone then made a sharp turn, raced the engine and roared off down the bumpy pasture, slowly lifting up into the morning sky with the little man now letting out all kinds of yelps.

Everyone was gawking up as the little aeroplane soared overhead and out over the fields and houses. It then made several circles, climbing higher and higher. Then, low and behold, down it came, roaring straight for the ground! Mercy, just as quickly up it went, turning completely upside down and roaring back down toward us as we started scrambling to get out of the way. Just when we thought it might crash, Capt. Ray B. made it zoom right over our heads as we could hear him laughing and the little man yelling. Finally the aeroplane went out a little ways, making one more sharp turn before coming back down to earth for a bumpy ride across the park pastureland.

SNAG & ME – A FLYING IN A JENNY   145

As soon as it came to a stop, the little man jumped and scampered for the gate as everyone was laughing. What a show this was turning out to be.

When one aeroplane had stopped, then one of the other pilots would load up somebody and it would zoom off into the sky. Some women even got into them, including our one an only teacher Mrs. Thrasher. You could hear them hollering even over the roar of the engines. As they flew overhead, they'd wave down at us. Even though I was not about to get into one of them things, I was thinking it would be something to see the ground from way up there in the sky where the buzzards flew.

CHRIS SHOWS US THE ROPES ABOUT AIRSHOWS

Chris yanked our arms and broke the spell of all this excitement. He took us straightaway to where the big trucks were parked, showing us the inside of these large trucks. He said they were "RIOS" and were very powerful. He also said that riding a long time in them wasn't too kind to your sitting down place. He had a special cushion that he sat on. Then he explained that a lot of times he would sleep inside the truck because it was more comfortable than in the tents on and old cot.

We met some of the other fellers who worked with them on these long trips. He showed us lots of tools and spare parts, as he called them, which they used to keep these aeroplanes going.

Then he showed us their 'Rolling Chuck Wagon.' This is where they stored all their eat'n stuff and cooking pans and such they used on their trips.

It sure looked interesting and also looked like a lot of hard work. I didn't think I would ever want to do

146   JOSEPH A. JOHNSTON

this even if I did get to see the aeroplanes all the time for free.

Next we got to meet Chris's grandpa again. This time he was much friendlier to us than when we first met. He was even smiling for a change.

"Hi fellers, welcome to the show. Now you boys don't know how much I really 'preciate you taking care of my Little Trooper here yesterday. He's my main little man an' I really make use of him a lot. He's sorta like an extra right arm at times. But I felt like he needed some time off. My prayers were answered when you fellers offered to show him around your place an' have a little fun too. That was just one big blessing, yes sir, it truly was. I know he gets tired of my bellyaching all the time, so thanks to you both again."

We both told him he was welcome and that we really enjoyed having Chris over to our places for a visit. We also told him how Chris had whupped us in about everything we tried. This caused his old Grandpa to really let out a hee-haw.

"Yep," he replied, "He's sort of sneaky about how he whups folks with all these games and things he knows about. Generally when he asks a question, the little rascal already knows the answer! You have to watch him from time to time. He's forever pulling one on me and the boys here. He can outshoot any of them with that fancy slingshot of his."

We both hollered at the same time, "Boy you can say that again!"

Mr. Sparks continued talking to us. "Hey, one other thing too while I got on my feeble mind. Chris tells me that one of your moms made that great blackberry pie he brought in yesterday evening."

I barked out, "That was my Mama who made the pie, Mr. Sparks."

SNAG & ME – A FLYING IN A JENNY   147

"Well, you tell her she did a mighty fine job an' it liked to have been a fight around here trying to get a piece of it before the rest of this greasy crew hawged it all. So, please tell your folks thanks a lot for the pie and for taking care of my little trooper for a day."

We both replied at the same time telling Mr. Sparks that it was all our pleasure and just wished Chris could hang around here forever.

His grandpa just smiled at us as he explained, "Well, that's a nice offer an' I'm sure the little trooper would love to hang around awhile longer. How some ever, if I don't get him on a train and headed back toward Tampa pretty soon, his folks will probably be ready to lynch me up to a tree when they see me."

We all laughed at Mr. Sparks and he was laughing right along with us.

WE MEET SOME MORE DARING AVIATORS

Chris then took us to see one of the other aeroplanes and to meet the aviators too. The first aviator was a well-dressed fellow and Chris told us his name was 'Baron Von Thistle.' He came over from Switzerland to America. He had been a flyer in the big war too, but said he never had to do any shooting at other aeroplanes. His plane had a name too: *Alpine Queen*. It was painted bright red.

Baron Von Thistle was a tall feller and spoke strange words mixed with a little English as he told us about his flying machine. We were having a hard time understanding everything he said but we did hear the part where he told us how much better he was at being an aviator than any of the aviators here. Mercy, he was starting to sound like Capt. Ray B. Ricker

MEETING A LADY DAREDEVIL

When we got finished with Baron Von Thistle, he shook our hands and wanted to know if we cared to go for a ride, telling us he was willing to let us ride for just two dollars apiece, if we didn't tell everyone about it.

We all laughed as Snag reminded him how poor we were. "Mr. Baron Von Thistle sir, we're so poor we can't pay 'tention an' you juss well ask for a hunnert dollars, cause money to us is only words. We never see the real thing."

The Baron got tickled at us as we waved bye. Chris was dragging us on to see the last little aeroplane. We met another aviator by the name of Mr. Warren LaBost. This man seemed like a nice feller too. Like Capt. Ray B. and the Baron, he showed us all the things about his little plane. The name on the side of his aeroplane was "SKY MASTER." There was one big difference in this plane. It had some special rigging up on the top wing. He was telling us that there was a lady who was part of the show and that she would be climbing up on top of the wing and sitting in a chair as he would fly this aeroplane around.

I knew right then that lady had to be crazy as a Betsy bug. Mercy, why would folks in their right minds do such crazy stunts?

We didn't have to wait long for an answer as about that time this handsome looking lady came walking up, dressed in leather britches, a fancy jacket with a silken scarf around her neck, and wearing an aviator cap with those odd looking spectacles. Chris told us those were called 'goggles.'

We learned that her name was Daring Dolly Dooley. Here we got to meet another famous person as she shook hands with us, telling us all about why she loved the thrill of this sort of work.

SNAG & ME – A FLYING IN A JENNY   149

Maybe it might have been exciting for her, but to me, I would have had fourteen heart attacks way before it ever got off the ground. She smiled real pretty like as she spoke to us and she was wearing some fancy smelling stink water too. Whew, I never smelled anything like that before. Snag was sniffing like a dog on a trail of a raccoon as she walked around us.

"Fellows, I'm real happy to meet you and to know that you all are special friends to Little Chris here. You know this little man never meets a stranger. I liked him the first time I ever saw him 'cause he was so sweet and kind to not only me, but everyone around here. He's always leaving me notes of encouragement with those little round faces on them. I always know who sent me a note as soon as I see that little round smiling face he draws on about everything around here. I think he and I will be friends from here to heaven and back."

This got Chris to blushing and us to giggling as the lady told us more about what was going to happen in a few minutes.

She smiled real pretty as she told us about what she was going to be doing on top of that aeroplane. "It may look scary to you here on the ground, but not to worry. I'm pretty well tied in up there and so there's no chance of me falling off. So keep that in mind. I'll be doing a few tricks, but I don't want to tell you all of it or else it won't be exciting for you to see. Now if one of you'd like, you can come along for the ride…but you'll have to ride up there with me!"

We backed away; for sure I didn't want a part of that kind of flying. Even Snag didn't want a ride if he had to sit on top of a wing with very little to hang onto.

She looked at us with a wide grin on her face. "Well, fellers, I take it none of you want to go for a ride with me. Okay, I'll go sadly alone. Now we'll be starting our

150 JOSEPH A. JOHNSTON

little act here in just a few minutes. So, how about you all hanging around here with Chris because we'll be taking off very soon. I'll do some tricks on that aeroplane that I bet you've never seen before."

This caused us to smile real big as Snag replied, "Oh Missus Dooley, shoot fire, we ain't saw this many flying machines all together before… so anything we see from now on is like icing on a cake!"

The lady just smiled as she patted Snag on the back and then she prepared to climb up on the aeroplane wing.

I poked Snag. "Snag, you reckon she's ready for the funny farm?" He and Chris both looked at me and giggled as we watched her climb on top of that aeroplane. Then the aviator climbed inside the cockpit as Big Jim came running over to pull the propeller. But before he could get started, this other fellow with a straw 'Panama hat', stripped britches and a bright yellow jacket, was waving his hands all about, then placing this big pipe of a thing to his lips as he began hollering.

"Ladieeeeees and gentlemennnnnnn, may I have your kind attention. Please, if you would, kindly observe the little blue and white aeroplane behind me and take special notice of a young and beautiful lady sitting atop the wing. She just happens to be none other than the famous and daring young lady from Dallas, Texas; the one and only; 'Daring Dolly Dooley.' Let's give her a big round of applause!"

Well, we and everyone around there that was watching, all clapped our hands loudly and whistled and the like. Then the fellow with the stovepipe looking thing hollered again.

"Folks, now please pay close attention or else you will miss some of the action. So let's all watch her daring and dangerous feats as she will astound you with her

SNAG & ME – A FLYING IN A JENNY   151

artistic ways of bravery while riding on top of this aeroplane as it does loops, rolls, spins, all to frighten even the most steadfast person. Now those with weak hearts, you best turn your heads and the ladies that are subject to fainting, you best get the smelling salts ready for this little act will take your breath away. As in the past, Miss Dooley appreciates your prayers for her safety… Thank you and kindly observe this magnificent act of aerial bravery."

In just a few minutes the little plane was roaring down the pasture and up into the sky. It began flying around in circles with this lady hanging on for dear life, or so it seemed to us. Then she would lay down on one side, then the other and look like she was going to fall off, but didn't. The plane roared higher and higher and then came roaring down toward us and then just as quickly up it went and over on it's back and back at us again. It was pure amazing, that lady was still hanging on! I was nervous as a cat and Snag was drooling at the mouth. Now she was standing up flatfooted as that aeroplane went into another one of those high loops.

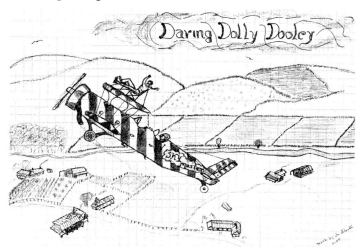

152 Joseph A. Johnston

Snag poked me in the sides. "Boy, Earl D., you know, after thinking about that kind of a ride, I think I'd like to try that myself!"

At that very moment, I knew my old pal had lost his cotton-picking mind. "Snag, you heard me say something about that lady may be ready for the funny farm... I think you and her both are ready."

That comment didn't even set him off like some things I say to him. Well, I guess he was struck by the sight of all this. To me it was just a bit more than scary.

We watched closely as the little plane did several rollovers, circles, ups and downs and around all over the place, and some real close to the ground. Finally it came back down for a landing, bouncing across the pasture as everyone let out a big round of clapping and hollering. This lady was waving all the way in and quickly jumped down and took a bow. Many folks were running up to her to shake her hand, asking a thousand questions and some even wanted her to write her name on a piece of paper. There was more clapping and whistling. I had to admit, she was either a very brave or a very crazy lady. Chris said that she was real brave. I had to agree to part of that.

SNAG GOES A LITTLE CRAZY ON ME

Snag had begun acting in a strange way. He was really excited over all the commotion of folks riding in the aeroplanes. Especially after watching Miss Daring Dolly Dooley do her stuff on top of that aeroplane. He kept wishing he had three dollars. I reminded him, we couldn't even scrape up a quarter a piece to get in the park, much less three whole dollars!

"Snag, if you kindly recall we didn't have a red cent between us yesterday and you know what else?"

SNAG & ME — A FLYING IN A JENNY   153

He looks at me with that crazy grin… "Naaa, what else, Earl D.?"

I laughed. "Well, in case you haven't noticed, Mr. Snag, we still don't have a red cent between us. If you think about it, if we hadn't of helped Capt. Ray B. out and having a little more luck meeting up with Chris here, we'd still be outside of the park looking in."

That didn't keep Snag from scheming and trying to figure out how he could get a free ride in one of them Flying Jennies! Suddenly, he grabbed my arm and started pulling me toward Capt. Ray B.'s aeroplane. Now this gave me a frightened look and thoughts to go with it, causing Chris to giggle a little bit, wondering I suppose what was going on inside Snag's pea brain head.

"Come on, Chris, Earl D.," he yelled. "I'm gonna ask Capt. Ray B. for a free ride."

I pulled loose and yelled out at my old pal. "Whoa, Snag, hold yore horses. I ain't being no part of this scheme of yours this time. Tain't no way Capt. Ray B. is gonna let you fly in that aeroplane an' if'n he did, yore pa would whup you till you hurt into next year and then some!"

He stopped pulling for a moment, but only long enough to yell back at me.

"Earl D., whupping or no whupping, this here is my chance to fly an' I'm a-gonna ask Capt. Ray B. to please give us a ride!"

I quickly grasped his last comment. "What'd ya mean *us*? I ain't a gonna get nowhere near that aeroplane with it running. Snag I think you've lost your mind for sure!"

Chris was taking all this in and looking worried a bit too. I guess he was a bit surprised at Snag's idea too. Now Snag looked at me rather sad, even Skip looked at me dejected as Snag hung his head slightly, giving me

154 JOSEPH A. JOHNSTON

that sadder than sad look he can sometimes get when he's wanting something special.

"Earl D., all I'm asking you to do is at least go with me. Who knows, Capt. Ray B. may run us both off, but I gotta ask him 'cause I don't have no three dollars an' if you 'member, we did him a big favor."

Giving in, I eased on down the slope as Chris joined. We walked as slow as I could manage because I didn't like to think of what was running through Snag's mind and mostly because the bells were ringing in my head as I remembered Mama's fateful words about not letting Snag get me into any kind of trouble. Now I felt like a lamb being led to slaughter... this was causing me to feel just a little sick at the moment.

We sidled up close to the aeroplane where Capt. Ray B. and Mr. Sparks were talking more kindly to one another than they were the other day when they seemed like they wanted to kill each other.

Snag didn't waste any time getting to the point. "Capt. Ray B., I gotta ask you a big favor...sorta like you asked of me and Earl D. the other day."

SNAG TALKS HIS WAY INTO GETTING US BOTH IN TROUBLE

Capt. Ray B., with a look of surprise on his face, looked at Snag, then at me and then at Chris. Then he glanced down at Skip who was wagging his tail like it was no tomorrow. Removing his big cigar and letting loose a cloud of rich smoke, he spoke in his gravely sounding voice.

"Okay fellers, what is it you got on your minds?"

I was trying to mumble that I didn't have anything to do with this, but Snag blurted out what he had on his mind instead.

SNAG & ME – A FLYING IN A JENNY   155

"Capt. Ray B. sir," Snag began, "You know we're pore'n a snake an' we couldn't get three dollars if'n they were free! So, all's we're asking of you kindly an' purty please is to take us for a ride in this machine an' we'd be mighty beholding to you for the rest of our lives. If'n you did us this one small favor, we'd be obliged forever."

I was about as surprised as Capt. Ray B. as I began to utter my displeasure of not wanting anything to do with a aeroplane ride. Capt. Ray B. with his mouth hanging open and now Mr. Sparks came to life as he began laughing out loud. I wasn't expecting what was to come out of this.

Capt. Ray B. took in a long breath, looking around and then back at us. "I tell you what, fellers, I'll give you a ride right after dinner when the crowd will probably thin out a bit. But, I don't want to let you ride unless your folks give me the OK."

Snag wasn't going to let this pass either. "Awwww shucks, Capt. Ray B., my pa wouldn't let me ride in a aeroplane if'n I owned it lock stock an barrel. Capt. Ray B. sir, ain't you always heard, it's a heap better to get forgiveness than permission?"

This only caused Capt. Ray B. to chuckle a little louder. "Young feller, I tell you one thing, if you survive until you get grown, you ought to get into politics."

Snag had that puzzled look on his face. "What's politics?"

Capt. Ray B. smiled. "Well, Snag, if you don't know, then it's too complicated to tell you what it's all about in one setting. My advice is that you just hang on and manage to get grown and it'll all come natural."

With that Capt. Ray B. and Mr. Sparks, both laughing a little at Snag I was sure, walked off toward a tent of sorts where there was coffee and the like.

CHRIS LETS US KNOW ABOUT TRUE FRIENDSHIP

I was starting to get real upset with my lifelong friend for including me in on this crazy notion of flying around Blanchard Forks in a smoking, noisy contraption that has a habit of falling out of the sky!

"Snag", I yelled, "I already told you I ain't gonna get into that flying machine for nobody and that includes you! Now you know doing something dumb like this would cause my folks to run me off for being just an out an' out bad son for disobeying their word. No sir, I ain't interested no matter what you say or do."

The argument got worse and I was beginning to think this was the end of us being pals, going fishing, telling tall tales and enjoying the world around us. That caused some deep, heart-felt thinking and for sure this kind of talk didn't set well with me. I even thought maybe somewhere in that empty head of his, Snag was thinking the same thing. Even Chris was seeing how upset I was about this as he began trying to calm us both down.

"Snag, Earl D.," he started, "Now I think you two fellers shouldn't get cross with one another over this aeroplane business. How's about calming down a bit and think it over what is going on here. If it's what your folks may do to you if you take a ride in Capt. Ray B's aeroplane, then maybe you better think it might be wiser to forget about it and just enjoy the fact you got to see the planes up close. You got to meet the folks who fly in them too."

We both stood there as Chris continued to give us a good lesson about friendship.

"Now I can tell you that true friendship is supposed to last forever and that includes heaven! So you have to think real serious like how much you treasure each other's friendship 'cause I tell you, I may be young and all that, but one thing I know for sure and that is, true friendship ain't cheap, though it's free. You pay through being understanding with one another, watching what you say and how you act too. There's always a lot of give and take... but with true friends, it's mostly giving. True friends are like diamonds, rare and worth more than gold. Now on the other hand, selfish friends are like quick silver...run right through your life and just when you need them to hang around, they're gone. Just like that, that's the end of it.

Chris took a long deep breath as Snag and me were starting to feel like a couple of polecats for sure. Chris started in on us again.

"The way you two are acting, your friendship is in trouble and it might not weather another storm. So you both need to reconsider the other's feelings and remember, there will be other chances to have some excitement in your lives… including maybe riding in an aeroplane someday. Who says it has to be today?"

Snag was moaning now… "Chris, I hear what you say an all, but I tell you the gospel, I doubt if'n I'll ever have a chance to ride in one again if'n I let this'un pass me by."

Chris just shook his head like he was a bit put out with Snag's remarks. Now I was worried we had just lost a friend, and we had just got him.

WE REPAIR OUR NEARLY BROKE FRIENDSHIP

I was standing there with my mouth ajar listening to Chris tell us more on how important friendship was. Mercy, what a smart little feller he was. I know Snag was standing there too, numb-struck and for once in his life, he didn't know how to answer what Chris had

158   JOSEPH A. JOHNSTON

been talking about. Mostly the other answer he gave wasn't fitting. Finally he broke the silence as Chris stood there looking at us both, I guess to see what would happen next.

"All right, Earl D." Snag replied, "If'n you don't want to ride an' Capt. Ray B. says he'll take me by myself, then that's the way it'll be. I want us to stay friends 'cause I rather be friends with you than any of the other fellers here about. So, don't worry, I won't ask you no more!"

With that last exchange, few words were said between us. I was wondering if Snag really took it to heart what all Chris had said, or was he just being bone headed anyway.

We walked around with Chris, looking over the aeroplanes again and the large trucks that were part of this aeroplane show. The big rubber tires, all the pedals, gauges and gear levers were real interesting to us since we had never seen one of these type trucks up close until today.

One of the fellers that worked with the show and drove one of the trucks from here to there, told us a few more things about the trucks and how powerful they were. This was just like Chris had told us earlier. I was convinced that Chris knew about everything there was to know. The other feller told us that these trucks could go over the back roads in daylight or dark better than a twenty-mule team and pull twice as strong!

Turning to Snag, who was still down in the draw over our little disagreement, I made a stab at breaking the silent treatment he was giving me.

"You know, Snag, I'd bet one of these trucks could be real handy around our place, then ole Charlie wouldn't have such a niche carved out with our family. Papa could sell him off quick, except, I doubt if this

SNAG & ME – A FLYING IN A JENNY   159

truck could do much plowing, and I'd miss old Charlie for sure!

"Yeah," yelped Snag, "besides ole Charlie is much cheaper to operate. He eats hay an' I betcha this here truck couldn't go very far on a bale of hay!" With that he gave one of his crazy laughs that got Chris and everyone around us laughing at Snag and his style of laughing. Maybe he was over his being upset with me.

Finally we spotted Capt. Ray B. back down near his aeroplane as he motioned for us to come down where he was. Snag broke into a fast run, pulling Skip along with the rope. Poor Skip, not being used to this sort of treatment, was putting up a good fight, but Snag wasn't slowing down, he just dragged Skip along anyway.

Chris and I walked slowly, but I knew in my bones that Snag was going to try his best to trick me into flying around in this machine anyway, no matter what Chris or I said.

CAPT. RAY B. MAKES US A DEAL

As we gathered in front of the aeroplane, Capt. Ray B. looked down at us. It seemed he might have changed his mind, but I was surprised when he said, "Fellers, here's the deal, Either you all three get a free ride or none of you get a free ride. What's it gonna be?" With that he stooped over us with his cigar really going, covering us with smoke as he blew out a whole belly full of it!

Coughing and sputtering, Snag looked at me with what seemed like a tear in his eye and his lips quivering. He mumbled, "Earl D., if'n we miss this here chance, we'll never have another an' you know it!"

I looked at him, then at Chris, who was looking more than a little uneasy at Snag's latest outburst. Then

160   JOSEPH A. JOHNSTON

Capt. Ray B. started laughing and grinning like a mule eat'n briers. I was thinking that if we, meaning Chris and I, didn't go, then there would be no riding at all and he wouldn't have to worry about us. Now I was between a rock and a hard place...even Skip was sulking.

"Snag," I said, "You know when our pa's find out about this, we gonna get a skinning like never before an' we'll probably never get to go fishing again or anywhere else till we're grown an' out on our own!"

Snag with a slow grin in his face looked at me close. "Does that mean you'll go too, Earl D.?"

"Yeah, I reckon so, but only if Chris can go too," I muttered as though it was doomsday.

"All rightttttttt!" Snag yelled as he jumped up and down. He quickly drug poor Skip off to tie him to a tree. In nothing flat he was back breathing fast and smiling big as ever.

Chris had a nervous smile, which told me he wasn't too sure he wanted to ride in an aeroplane either. We thought maybe he had gone flying before, since he'd been traveling with his grandpa and going to these air shows for some time now. But we soon found out he hadn't been up in one of those aeroplanes yet either. In a way, I was hoping his grandpa might tell him flat out that he wasn't going... then I would be free to make like I was sad that the whole thing didn't work out, and it wouldn't be my fault.

"Chris, you think your grandpa will let you fly around in this contraption with us?" I asked with a worried tone of voice.

Chris looked around and then explained his side of the story. "Fellows, I'm not sure, but if that's the only way Snag can have his dream come true, I'll go ask and see what my grandpa says. It depends on how much trust he has in Capt. Ray B. today."

SNAG & ME — A FLYING IN A JENNY   161

With that, Chris darted off to find his grandpa. Shortly, they were back and his grandpa didn't seem too happy, as he and the Capt. got into it again.

MR. SPARKS HAS SOME BAD THOUGHTS

"Ray B., you crazy jackass! Have you lost your mind trying to tell these boys they can fly with you, and knowing their folks would be more than a little upset once they find out? You could get yourself hung to a tree, or shot!"

Capt. Ray B. just leaned back against the little plane named Angel Wings and let more smoke come out of his cigar.

"Now listen, you old coot, I ain't worried 'bout their folks. I'm good at this bizness an' flying is like breathing to me, so I'll take a chance and give the lads a ride they'll remember for the rest of their lives. Now how about you? You gonna let Little Chris come along or are you gonna knock all three of them out of a chance to have a little excitement?"

I watched Chris and then his grandpa. Then I looked strongly at Snag trying to make him think what a jam he was putting all of us into and how tough it was for Mr. Sparks to say yes or no. I guess Snag wasn't thinking about what may happen to us either up there in the sky someplace or after we get back down if the Good Lord lets us. I watched the expression on Mr. Sparks face, hoping he would say NO and then I'd be free of this mess Snag was getting us into.

I was already silently praying and asking God to forgive me for being such a bad son to my folks, but also telling Him that it's because of my friend with a pea brain that I'm about to do the dumbest thing in my

162 JOSEPH A. JOHNSTON

life. Then I was telling Him how I wish He had given me more brains so I could've talked my way out of this!

Chris's grandpa sure didn't like this situation, as he looked down at Chris with a hard look on his face. "Little Trooper, how come you get me in this miserable mess anyway? If I let you do this crazy thing, how in heavens name am I gonna explain this to your mom and dad when I see them again? You know they're gonna be twice times upset—especially your mom. She's just feisty enough to poke me in the nose if she thinks I let you do something you shouldn't."

Chris just smiled. "Grandpa, the ride will be just a short one and I won't tell my folks unless you do. It'll be our secret."

Mr. Sparks looked really down in the draw. "Now, you know good and well I never hide anything from your folks, and so we'll tell them proper like so there won't be no secrets between us. I know they're gonna hate my guts for awhile."

IT LOOKS LIKE WE ARE GOING FOR A RIDE IN THE SKY

Chris grabbed his grandpa and hugged his neck. "Awww, Grandpa, it's gonna be all okay and I don't think Mom and Dad will stay upset with you for very long. They'll be so happy to see me that this little adventure won't even come to mind."

Mr. Sparks looked woefully at us and muttered, "Now all I gotta do is pray that this thing gets up and back in one piece and Lord forgive me for even letting this happen. Ray B. you scallywag, you know if I allow Chris to go up with you in that machine, you best fly this thing like you've never flown before and no funny stuff either while you're up there. I want you to get up there and back in one piece. Make it just a short haul and I expect you back in just a short bit... got that?"

Capt. Ray B. was giggling. "Awww, quit your worrying, old timer. I'll make it safe and easy for the boys. All I want to do is give them the sensation of being off the ground and up in the air. That's all. No loops, no funny stuff. That okay with you?"

Mr. Sparks stared at him and then at us. "Yep, that's all I want you to do. I think I'll just get on my knees right now and start praying until you all get back down on the ground, all in one piece. Now get in there and let's get this misery over with quickly."

I was nearly in tears as Capt. Ray B. helped us climb in, taking some straps with big brass buckles, tying us in so tight we could hardly wiggle. Three of us in one seat. I was shaking so hard that my teeth, knees, eyeballs and hair was shaking. I looked around at Snag and he was grinning like crazy, but shaking as bad as I was. Chris was in the middle and hanging on to both of us. This meant we were all flat scared to death. I voiced my opinion one more time.

"Snag, you know we're all crazy as loons for doing this!"

"Yeah, I reckon so," he replied, "But ain't this the most excit'n thing you've ever done earl D? Shucks, we'll be able to tell our grandkids about this someday an' they'll probably laugh like crazy!" He started laughing again.

I gritted my teeth. I wasn't laughing. I felt more like undoing this belt around me and high-tailing it for home, friend or not. "Yes, Mr. Snag, that is if we get back in one piece—and remind me to hate you for a month or two."

Chris gave me that serious look again. "Awwww, Earl D., you don't mean that."

164 JOSEPH A. JOHNSTON

Before I could answer him Capt. Ray B. got our attention.

"Okay fellers, see this heah tube and funnel looking thing?"

"Yep, we shore do, Capt. Ray B.," Snag replied.

"Well," Capt. Ray B. began to explain, "If you want to yell at me while we're flying, you gotta yell through that thing and I'll hear you and talk back to you. But, yell only if you having a serious problem like throwing up or something like that."

Now I got real scared. "Capt. Ray B., you mean we gonna get sick in this thing and throw-up all over the place?"

Capt. Ray B. was laughing as he answered my last question. "Not all the time, but some folks get in here and get sicker'n a ole mule at plow'n time, but that don't mean you fellers will get sick. In case you do, there's a little hole on both sides. Try and aim for that so it won't be so messy. If you get sick, then you fellers will have to clean it up. Now don't get sick!"

With that, he climbed into the cockpit behind us as Mr. Sparks checked us out one more time, moaning about letting Chris go with us on this adventure of a lifetime. After looking at Chris real close, I guess still questioning whether to let him go or not, he slowly reached over and squeezed Chris's arm. He then turned and gave Capt. Ray B. a harsh look and muttered something under his breath about Capt. Ray B. being crazy as a rabid skunk as he walked around in front of the aeroplane.

"All right, you crazy jackass—CONTACT!"

WE'RE OFF AND FLYING IN A REAL AEROPLANE

With a couple of loud grunts he gave the propeller a real hard pull and the engine fired up. Mercy! It was

SNAG & ME – A FLYING IN A JENNY   165

really noisy so close to this thing. It shook so bad I thought it was going to fall apart right there on the ground…with us in it!

Snag, Chris and I were hanging on to each other for dear life as it roared off down the pasture, bouncing, with smoke blowing everywhere. Finally I felt it rise, too scared to even look out.

Snag peeped out the little side hole. Seeing the ground disappearing below us, he couldn't contain his emotions. "Earl D., Chris, would ya look-a there! We're flying. We're really flyinggggggggg! Yeaaaaa hoooooo… boy, this is funnnnnnn I'm tell'n you the gospel."

I was shaking so bad and praying some more as I loudly reminded Snag of something in the future. "Snag you better say a prayer too that we get back down on the ground in one piece 'cause our pa's gonna tear us to pieces when they find out about this!"

"Aw shucks, Earl D.," he yelled over the engine noise. "Quit yore worry'n an' enjoy this excitement. Shoot-fire, I betcha our pa's would probably ride too if'n they had a half a chance. 'Sides, what's a little ole whupping? Heck fire, we'll be good as new in a day or two!"

I wasn't convinced, but with a lot of courage on my part, I managed a look out over the edge of the cockpit as Capt. Ray B. tilted the aeroplane over, scaring me even more as it went up and down and bounced around. I looked down, feeling a little dizzy, I could see all over Blanchard Forks in one look! I had never seen this much of our place even from the mountaintop. I had to admit this was exciting, and about the most nerve-shaking thing I had ever done in my life. I could hardly think for the roar of the engine, but I told myself that I best remember it all real good because I don't think I will ever do it again, friend or no friend!

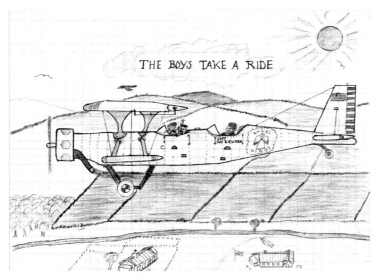

Snag was pointing out our houses. "Looooooookkkkkk, Earl D., there's yore house... an'....an'....lookeee over there, there's my house. Hey, would ya lookee there, I can see some of my brothers an' sisters outside in the front yard just a waving at us!"

I struggled to grab his hand but couldn't reach it. All I could do was yell, "Don't wave back, you mule head! They'll run in and tell your ma an' pa and we'll get that licking 'fore we get back down on the ground good!

"Aw, Earl D., they can't see that far and tell who it is!"

"Well," I yelled over the engine noise. "They just might recognize us and so don't wave. The way we're yelling, they can probably hear us and know who it is anyway!"

CHRIS GETS A LITTLE GREEN IN THE GILLS

Chris was sitting between us and not saying much. Now I was feeling sorry for him. "Chris, you okay?"

SNAG & ME – A FLYING IN A JENNY 167

He looked as me like he was just a tad on the woozy side. "Earl D., I think I'm about half sick of this aeroplane ride already."

Snag jerked around. "Chris, now look, don't go get'n sick on us. Shoot, we'd have to clean this thing up and that wouldn't be no kinda fun, would it?"

Chris shook his head as he tried to ease over near one of the little openings. He was sucking in some air and making deep breaths. We watched him closely, hoping he wouldn't throw up. After we bounced around some more and a few deep breaths, he leans back against the seat. Now he didn't look so green in the gills this time, as he gives us a happier smile. "I think what I needed was a couple of good draws on some fresh air. The smoke and smells of this thing makes you sort of sickly. I think I'll make it now."

We both patted him on the back and thanked him for not throwing up.

By that time we were way out over the woods, past the town. We could see Fletcher's creek below and the tall mountains off to the side of us. Chris was straining to look out the holes and we were all just staring at everything. Snag and me had managed to wiggle up high enough to look over the edges of the seat real good. I guess I best remember all this real good cause like it or not, it'll probably be the last time for me.

Capt. Ray B. yelled at us through that funny looking pipe. "Hey, you fellers okay up there?"

Sang grabbed the tube and yelled back, "Yes sir, Capt. Ray B., we're fine as frog hair an' we ain't throwed-up yet!"

This only caused Snag to start laughing like a hyena. I was wondering if he ever got scared of anything. I knew as scared as Chris and I were, we couldn't help but make a nervous giggle too.

GETTING READY TO LAND AND STILL IN ONE PIECE

Capt. Ray B. turned the aeroplane some, causing the plane to go up and down, bouncing around like a rubber ball. I thought on several turns we were gonna go upside down. If that happened I knew that Chris and I would both get sick for sure! But finally, my prayers were answered. Capt. Ray B. yelled out us again, "Okay fellers, we're going back down, so hang on!"

With that Capt. Ray B. made a sharp turn and I nearly lost my breath and everything inside of me. Chris was hanging on tightly now as Snag must have had some of the same feelings as he hollered out, "Whew boy, it's good thing I didn't eat a bunch of stuff 'fore this ride or else we'd have a shore-nuff mess on our hands."

I was watching Snag closely as he wiped his mouth with his sleeve, while taking deep breaths. Lordy, I thought... let's hurry and get back on the ground. I knew if one of us got sick, we'd all three be throwing up.

Then we got another big scare as we dropped like a rock, all three of us were grabbing a hold of each other. Snag gave me his first concerned look.

"Earl Deeeeeeee," he yelled. "You reckon Capt. Ray B. is trying to get to that big hanger in the sky already, an' taking us with him?"

I gulped some air real fast, trying to yell over the noise, with my shaking teeth and knees. "I shore hope not. I'll really miss Mama and her good cook'n, an' I'll miss Percy, an' Papa, even Nell Faye, an' Ole Charlie, an' we'll not grow up together Snag!"

I was admitting I was scared into tears at the thoughts of my life maybe coming to a tragic and sad

SNAG & ME – A FLYING IN A JENNY   169

end, especially dying doing something I ought not be doing! Chris was just staring straight ahead, and I guess thinking maybe this wasn't going to work out just right.

BACK ON THE GOOD EARTH AT LAST

Snag was about to yell at me when the plane smoothed out. Now we were much lower as we flew over some treetops, some fence rails and then it dropped again and this time before we could recover from our loss of breath, we were bouncing on the ground. With several bumps we finally pulled up to the spot where we had left. Capt. Ray B. shut off the loud engine. It sputtered, let a big popping sound, and came to a stop as the big propeller quit spinning.

With a large sigh of relief, Snag, Chris and I undid the belts that were holding us in and started climbing out, with all of us exclaiming that we'd had enough of these Flying Jennies for a while. What we didn't realize was that we had a surprise waiting on us.... A un-welcomed welcoming committee!

THE WELCOMING COMMITTEE IS WAITING ON US

Standing just a short distance away, near a small group of folks that were watching us return to the earth, was none other than our pa's! They spotted us immediately and both of them were heading right for us.

We had been taught never to run from our parents—well, me at least. I wasn't sure what Snag might do at any moment, but there we all three stood knowing that Snag and me were gonna catch it, but good. Chris stood there with us I guess to try and help explain why we did this dumbest trick of our lives to begin with.

Capt. Ray B., apparently realizing about this time that we were headed for trouble, came up quickly to our sides. With a comforting look, he promised to help persuade our pa's not to beat us within a inch of our lives.

He looked at Snag and asked, "What's your papa's name, son?"

Snag, scared at what was coming his way, stammered, "His name is Pa!"

Capt. Ray B. chuckled a bit, but asked again, "I mean his real name, son!"

"I told you, Capt. Ray B., his name is Pa—Pa Galloway!"

"All right, but don't he have a first name?"

"If'n he does, I don't know it, but it don't matter none, he's gonna kill me anyways!"

Sure enough, my papa, and Snag's pa were right there in a shake, telling us in a deathly serious tone of voice to follow them and get prepared for a double dose of a whupping!

We were about ready to follow them like sheep to a killing when Capt. Ray B. walked up to Papa and Mr. Galloway.

"Excuse me, fellers. Hold up just a minute while I try to explain all this. Mainly, don't take your hate for me out on the boys here. They wouldn't have went up in my machine if I hadn't practically begged them to. So if you gonna whup up on somebody, then you gotta whup up on me 'cause I'm the guilty party."

About that time Mr. Sparks and Big Jim showed up, seeing that trouble was a brewing. Now I was worried that my pa and Mr. Galloway might get in a fight of some kind. I didn't want that to happen for sure.

SNAG & ME – A FLYING IN A JENNY   171

Mr. Galloway and Papa stood there for a minute, a little bit of shock creeping into their faces seeing these other two folks join up with Capt. Ray B.

This didn't slow Papa down for he had something on his mind and no matter how many folks were around, he was going to have his say.

Looking first at Capt. Ray B., then us, Papa finally broke the staring spell.

"Mister, we don't know you and you had no right whatsoever to take our boys flying in that contraption of a machine. You could've all been killed!"

Capt. Ray B. smiled broadly as he calmly lit up his cigar again. Then just as calmly, he blew some smoke rings out. Mr. Sparks and Big Jim stood there watching what all was going on.

Capt. Ray B. then began to tell Papa and Mr. Galloway how good a aviator he was and how many times he'd been up flying all over the United States and France and had never had a serious crash. He was talking really fast, so as to prevent Papa and Mr. Galloway a chance to holler at him about his latest flying feat, and hopefully saving us a licking.

PAPA GETS SERIOUS AS CAPT. RAY B. OFFERS THEM A GOOD DEAL

Papa was about up to his ears in all this as he raised his hand to ask for a chance to say something, but Capt. Ray B. made one more gesture to change their minds about our overdue punishment.

"Look fellers, while we're resting here, I need to tell you that my name is Captain Ray B. Ricker and I'm about the best aviator around. Now those aren't just empty words, them are facts! Now I'm deeply sorry you feel so upset about me carrying your boys for a

172 JOSEPH A. JOHNSTON

short ride, but if you could've seen the look in their eyes when they learned they had a chance to fly in a real aeroplane, you would've cried! I wouldn't have dared let them fly with me if I wasn't as good as I say I am. Now I'll try to prove all this to you two fine gentleman."

There was more staring as Papa was about to say something, but again, Capt. Ray B. got to going. "Fellers, first I know you both are a pair of caring and concerned papa's to these fine boys. By the way, they helped me out of a mess the other day, so's partly I owed them a little something to show my gratitude. Now I propose a deal you fellers can hardly refuse. I'll gladly fly one or both of you up for a free ride just to show you how safe it is and the excitement of buzzing with the angels up there in God's blue sky. I think you'll quickly change your minds about this whole mess."

I had to shake my head a bit, listening to Capt. Ray B.'s explanation about his ability to fly that machine. He was good, that's for sure—not only of being a good aviator but telling good tales to save the likes of Snag and me.

As I watched Papa and Mr. Galloway squirm and wiggle, I wondered what their answer would be. I still marveled at Capt. Ray B., in this case, his storytelling. Whether it was stretching the truth a little till it had about all it could stand, didn't matter. It was certainly okay by Snag and me if it kept us from getting our sitting down places heated up from a razor strop!

Mr. Galloway was standing there with his mouth wide open and Papa with a frown on his face, scowling at Capt. Ray B. then at us. Papa finally relaxed his grip on my arm a bit. Boy that felt good.

Papa at last got a word in edgewise with Capt. Ray B. as he finally started talking again.

"Look mister, you can stop your preaching. I ain't gonna get in that contraption for you or anybody else! And let me tell ya something else. I don't care how good you are—or think you are—at flying that thing. One thing's for sure, my boy's gonna get his just punishment, 'cause he knew better than to ever pull a stunt like this!"

I felt his grip tighten on my arm again. I knew this meant we were on our way home... Well, nearly. But miracles happen and it looked like another one was in the making.

Just when Snag and I thought all was lost, Mr. Galloway touched Papa's arm and started talking a different tune.

"Jeb, didn't you hear what the man said?"

"Yeah, I heard what he said, and what are you trying to say?" Papa replied.

"Welllllll," Mr. Galloway began, now with a big grin on his face, "I ain't never known you to back down from a challenge, Jeb. Why, I thought you'd tangle tails with a wildcat if'n the challenge was laid on to yore doorstep."

Papa was becoming flustered at Mr. Galloway's remarks. Capt. Ray B., seeing the irritation build up a bit, proposed another approach.

"Look fellers, tell you what, let's be fair and square about this and toss a coin to see which one of you goes for a ride with me just to prove to you both that I'm as good as I say I am!"

Papa and Mr. Galloway stared at each other, both twisting around a bit to see us all staring at them wondering what was going to happen next. Papa surprised us with his next statement as he released my arm. Now that really felt good.

174 *JOSEPH A. JOHNSTON*

PAPA LOSES—OR WINS—THE FLIP OF A COIN

"Laroy, if you think I ain't man enough or brave enough to ride in that contraption you're crazy as your old milk cow bellerin' in a hailstorm. And, if you also think I'm scared to flip a coin on whether it's you or me, you're dead wrong there too!"

Mr. Galloway just saw a challenge laid on him too. Neither he nor Papa knew rightly how to get out of this latest turn of events short of letting Capt. Ray B. take one of them for a ride in his aeroplane. Capt. Ray B., smiling big, puffing away on a much shorter cigar, reached into his pocket and found a two-bit piece. Then he asked if they were ready to call the flip of the coin.

Papa reeled around and stated rather harshly, "Flip the stinking coin, mister, so we can get this mess over with! Laroy, it's gonna be fun watching you fly around up there screaming your head off."

"Well, Jeb, don't be so all fired sure," Mr. Galloway said. "Could be you up there and me down here laughing while you do some screamin'."

Capt. Ray B. took a big draw on his cigar. "Well, fellers since it appears neither one of you likes the idea of flying with me, tell you what let's do. If you call it right, then the other one is the loser and gets to fly with me." Then he asked one of them to call heads or tails. Papa immediately hollered out, "HEADS!"

Capt. Ray B. flipped the coin high into the air. All eyes were glued on it as it came down, hitting the dusty ground with a KERPLOP. As the dust cleared, Papa, Mr. Calloway and Capt. Ray B. gathered around the coin. Capt. Ray B. yelled out the news, "TAILS!"

Mr. Galloway was chuckling and even Snag broke into a grin. Papa had lost the toss of the coin! He got real red-faced and I knew he was upset. He didn't like losing at anything. Now this was really hard on him.

Now Mr. Sparks and Big Jim were all grins too, mostly because they felt that the chances of a ruckus were over and now they'd see how brave Papa was in the face of losing that coin toss.

With that, Capt. Ray B. announced to our little group, "All right, my friends, we're about to initiate another brave human into the sensational feeling of flying. We'll go sailing through the air without benefit of nothing more than my excellent flying skills as a humble, but great aviator at the controls of this marvelous mechanical invention. The sheer joy to break the bonds of the earth and soar like an eagle will make an imprint into your memories that will never get erased by anyone, except God. Of course, with God's great winds to assist us, it will be a total success!"

With that little speech made, he bowed low, then motioned Papa to the little aeroplane. We all walked down, listening as Capt. Ray B. explained all the rules of flying and how to speak through the tube; about how important it was to keep the belt good and tight around his waist. Papa, knowing his bravery was on the line and not wanting to look like a scardy cat, looked back at me with a sad look. I blurted out, "Papa, you're the greatest and most bravest Papa in the whole world and I'm proud to be your son!" He gave a halfhearted wave to me, as Mr. Sparks did his routine. In just a few grunts of pulling the propeller, once again the engine roared to life.

We watched as Capt. Ray B. turned the plane around with all the dust flying and in just couple of minutes they were off, bouncing up and down on the rough ground, finally lifting up and into the evening air they flew.

176   JOSEPH A. JOHNSTON

I was saying a silent prayer for Papa and for Capt. Ray B. too. I just wanted him to get safely back on the ground when I felt someone behind me grab my shoulders.

ANOTHER SURPRISE...WITH TERROR IN THEIR EYES

I spun around. There was Mama and Nell Faye, both breathing like they'd been in a foot race, crying and moaning that they would never see Papa alive again.

Nell Faye started yelling at me, "Earl D., why didn't you stop Papa from making a fool of himself? I'll tell you right now, if anything happens to Papa, it'll be all yore fault, Earl D., and God will take care of you!"

Just when I was feeling proud of Papa and his bravery, here's my sister telling me I wasn't no count and even Mama was upset at me, sobbing away as I tried to explain it all.

Mr. Galloway and even Little Chris tried to rescue me from the attacks from Nell Faye as Mama's tear-filled words hit me smack in the heart.

"Earl D., you oughta be so ashamed of yourself for enticing your poor Papa into getting into that awful flying machine."

Now she started crying even harder. Mr. Galloway took off his hat. With remorse in his voice, he explained that is was possibly his fault that Papa went up in the aeroplane and he was sorry that Jeb took him up on the challenge and lost a flip of the coin.

I touched Mama's arm and tried to assure her everything would be all right. "Mama, that Capt. Ray B. is a real fine aviator and I can swear by that, 'cause

Chris, Snag and me just got out of the aeroplane after Capt. Ray B. took us flying too!"

Mama collapsed right there on the ground as Nell Faye went into another screaming fit.

"Now look what you've done, Earl D, you idiot! You've killed your own Mama!"

With that she became totally hysterical as the crowds gathered around to gawk at us all and poor Mama laying there on the hot dusty ground.

I was convinced Nell Faye was right, worried about Mama and what to do in situations like this. I was scared; I had never been in a jam like this before. Luckily I spotted Ole Doc Pritchard as he came rushing up through the crowd that had gathered around my fallen Mama.

Over the years he had cared for the whole county, and probably was owed by everyone for all his visits and pills he passed out during those times. He took control of the situation real quick, telling everyone to move out as he grabbed Mama's wrist then raised her head a little. He yelled for someone to bring some cool water as he grabbed a fan from Mrs. Sweeny who was standing there gawking. Next thing you know Ms. Sweeny and her young'uns began singing a song that I guess she thought was proper at the time: *When the Roll Is Called Up Yonder*.

MAMA COMES BACK TO LIFE

Doc Pritchard quickly reached inside his coat pocket and drew out a bottle of something, then he slowly waved it under Mama's nose. In a just a few seconds Mama opened her eyes. Taking a sip of water, she looked around like she was still in a daze. Nell Faye was on her knees, all red eyed and thanking the Lord that she

178 JOSEPH A. JOHNSTON

was alive! I was too. Mercy, it wouldn't be any kind of life with our mama. Who would feed us?

Snag, scared out of his wits too, shook my arm. "Earl D., we gotta thank the Good Lord that yore mama's still kicking...I would've shore missed all them good dinners she makes." Little Chris was all red eyed too. I guess he too was glad Mama didn't pass on to heaven just yet.

As Doc Pritchard and Mr. Galloway helped Mama to her feet, she held on to his arm like she was still feeble of mind and body. Mrs. Sweeny and her family immediately started singing "I'll Fly Away". This caused the rest of the folks standing around to join in singing too and smiling again, knowing that Mama hadn't passed on to the promised land.

As Mama was dusting herself off, I was trying to say how sorry I was for all the problems I had caused her. "Mama, I'm so sorry this all happened an' I ain't smart enough to even try to explain it all, but if you like, I'll leave home forever an' become a hobo or go work in a traveling circus so you won't have to ever look at me anymore."

I hung my head down, about ready to start blubbering at the very thought of never seeing my family again, waiting for Mama to say it was okay for me to leave home.

WE ARE READY TO LEAVE HOME...BUT MAMA STOPS US COLD

Snag was standing beside me as he looked up at Mama then gave a little speech of his own.

"Missus McHenry, if'n the truth be known, then it's my time to tell the whole truth. It's all my fault from beginning to end. Every dadburn bit of it! You see, I

SNAG & ME – A FLYING IN A JENNY 179

nagged pore ole Earl D. into this whole thing. I begged him to ride in that aeroplane with me. I caused this whole stinking mess! I feel bad as all get-out about ever'thing an' if'n my Pa an' Ma feels badly 'bout me, then I'll go along with Earl D. an' we'll both be a couple of ole hobos. Maybe we'll even hitch up with a traveling circus too!"

Mama wiped the tears from her eyes and grabbed us both as Little Chris stood there beside his grandpa, who was trying to get a word in edgewise but held off for the moment. Mama looked at us both with words only a sweet Mama could say, and she said it to us.

"Earl D., Snag, Little Chris, you young fellers are just experiencing life and you are going at it so fast, that it overloads our senses at times. As grownups we get a bit scatter-brained when y'all do something new and different. Some things we'd never think of doing or be brave enough to even try. I don't want either one of you to ever leave home for any reason because that would surely break my heart and I would probably die for sure then. I know Little Chris's folks would miss him even more than they are now. So, Earl D., Snag, you both are special to me and my life would be pretty empty if I knew a couple of boys weren't around to keep me on my toes. If Little Chris lived around here, it would be the same for him. So, don't even think those kind of thoughts again! Now let us all pray that Papa and that aeroplane gets back down out of the sky in one piece!"

About that time Mr. Sparks introduced himself to Mama and tried to explain what all happened and why. Mama smiled nicely and told him not to worry about it. All that mattered now was for Papa to get back down on God's good earth in one piece.

180 *JOSEPH A. JOHNSTON*

OUR PRAYERS ARE ANSWERED...ANGEL WINGS MAKES A SAFE LANDING

Like magic, right over our heads zoomed Capt. Ray B. and his brightly colored aeroplane with Papa waving to us all from the front seat! I was excited as possum in a tree full of ripe persimmons, seeing Papa wave. This had to mean only one thing; he was having the time of his life flying in that aeroplane!

With no one looking, Chris, Snag and me shook hands behind everyone's back, all giggling and with a deep sigh of relief that perhaps there wouldn't be a severe whupping in store for Snag and me. It sure looked like we had possibly avoided the dreaded beating we thought for sure was coming our way.

The little aeroplane made a sharp turn way down at the end of the pasture and came down real smooth like, bouncing along over some of the ruts. Finally it pulled to a stop after bouncing a few times in the dust tracks it had worn out from so many ups and downs. Now we all anxiously waited as Papa slowly climbed out, then waited for Capt. Ray B. to get out. He had proven, not only to Papa and Mr. Galloway, but to everyone standing there watching him land that flying machine, that he was a world-famous aviator.

Capt. Ray B. wasn't expecting what was to follow. Papa actually reached out and shook his hand, thanking him for being a good aviator and getting them both back on the ground in one piece.

Capt. Ray B. let out a long and loud laugh. Then everyone in the little crowd laughed too. Mama and Nell Faye were quiet as they waited until Papa walked over.

"Jeb McHenry!" Mama began, "You and your son have scared us all out of our wits and I'm a nervous

SNAG & ME – A FLYING IN A JENNY   181

wreak over what you both have done to me this day. Even poor little Nell Faye is just about ready to faint from all this commotion. I think you owe us a little explanation!"

Papa, somewhat embarrassed by Mama's outburst in public, blushed bright red. He quietly reminded Mama that they would discuss it at home. With that he gently grabbed her arm and motioned for us to follow them out to the wagon. I begged Papa to let me tell Chris goodbye. He motioned for me to hurry it up.

TELLING CAPT. RAY B. AND CHRIS GOODBYE

I hurried back toward the aeroplanes to tell Chris goodbye. He let me know that they would be leaving the park tomorrow evening and that he'd like to see us again if possible. I told him that we'd try for sure.

Snag came running up beside me as I told him what Chris had said about leaving. "Snag, we just got to try and see our new pal one more time if our folks will let us an' I don't get a whupping after all this."

Snag reminded me that we were lucky so far and if what Mama had said meant anything, then we'd meet later on down at the swimming hole on Fletcher's creek.

Capt. Ray B., Mr. Sparks and Chris were standing there talking away. I smiled up at Capt. Ray B., who had another new cigar in his mouth, blowing lots of smoke and laughing. "Earl D., you trying to hog waller another free ride out of me?"

I had to laugh, as did Chris and Mr. Sparks. "No sir, I think I've had all the ridin' I want for a long time— and then some. What I want to do is thank you for getting Papa back down to the ground safely and for lettin' me, Chris an' Snag ride in your aeroplane."

182   JOSEPH A. JOHNSTON

He just laughed and said, "Next time, little feller, when I fall out of the sky, I hope it's another pair of good Samaritans like you and your friend, Snag, who come to my rescue. I couldn't have found a better set of helpers when I needed it."

Next, I told Chris we'd try to see him before he left tomorrow. I had a surprise from Chris. When I got ready to leave, he came up, shook my hand real strong like and gave me a bear hug too. Now this I wasn't used to, having a boy hug me—unless we were in a heated rasseling match.

"Earl D., you are what I call an instant friend and I wish we lived closer 'cause I'm sure we'd have lots of fun playing chess, marbles and the like. I might even learn how to milk your cow too!"

This caused all of us to laugh. "I don't know, Chris," I replied. "You're too smart for me to play any games with, an' I'm sure you'd be a world champion milker too if you go at it like everything else you do. But I'd still like for you to be our pal though you live way down in Tampa, Florida. We have your box number so we'll be sending you a letter once in awhile. How about that?"

He just grinned. "Yeah, maybe so. I'd enjoy reading a letter from you and Snag sometime. One thing, Earl D., just remember what I said about friendship."

"Oh, don't worry, Chris, I'll remember that the rest of my days and I'll always remember who told me about 'true friendship too. Thanks a lot."

I shook hands with his grandpa and Capt. Ray B, then turned and ran to catch up with my folks who were sitting in the wagon waiting for me. We all waved goodbye to them as Papa turned ole Charlie around and headed for the house. I waved and waved as Chris waved from the gate to the park. Yep, I was thinking, what a swell pal Chris is, even if he does live way down in Tampa, Florida.

The ride home was different. Every now and then an automobile passed us, causing a lot of dust. Also this new noise on the dirt road was causing ole Charlie to get down right skittish at times. In spite of all the dust and noise, we made it home in one piece. Mama said it would take two washings to get all the dust out of our hair and clothes. Now that didn't sound like much fun to me.

PAPA DOESN'T WIN ANY ARGUMENTS WITH MAMA

In the late evening, Mama and Papa were in the swing, both taking turns about saying 'why this and why that and don't ever again' which meant that Papa lost not only the flip of the coin, it was sounding like he was losing his argument with Mama too. He promised her he wouldn't ever go flying in one of those flying machines again.

They called me to the front porch. Percy had been prodding me to tell him all about it, but time was running out. I knew it was my turn to accept some tongue lashing from them both. I took it like a man. Papa finally admitted that perhaps he shouldn't have gone for a ride either, but then on second thought, he said, "Shoot, why not? I'm a grown man and it fit just right. So, Pearl, we'll just say we had a memory making day and be glad it all ended up well."

Mama didn't smile straight away, but in a few shakes, I noticed that smile creeping up on her face. Then I knew all was okay. The only burr under our saddle was Nell Faye. She was still quiet as a church

184   JOSEPH A. JOHNSTON

mouse walking on cotton and wouldn't say boo to any of us. Even Percy couldn't get her yakking.

I liked her being quiet; but then again, I worried about her being so upset. I thought perhaps I would try to get her yakking again... back to hollering at me... that would be normal. But I decided that keeping her quiet wasn't so bad. So, that coming back to normal could come later.

My punishment wasn't too bad considering it could have been a lot worse. My fishing time had been cut down to just three days a week. They also lined up a few more chores for me to do to gain my freedom back. This would last as long as they felt I needed it, and there would be no begging to break the rules.

MEETING SNAG AT THE SWIMMING HOLE

After promising to obey, I asked my parents if I could run down to the creek and meet Snag for a few minutes. They both looked at me. "Now Earl D., we just told you there would be no fishing. What are you going to be doing with Snag down there this time of day?" Mama asked.

"Oh, Mama, nothing special, just a little talking about seeing Chris off tomorrow if we can manage it and then I'll head straight back to the house, I promise."

Papa wasn't saying anything, leaving all the talking to Mama. "Well, you can go, but you have to take Percy with you, and get back quick 'cause I'm warming up what was left from dinner. And when you head back, better bring in some more wood for the stove."

I nodded as I ran into the house to get Percy up from the bed where he was taking a nap. He was excited as I told him we were going down to the creek to meet

SNAG & ME – A FLYING IN A JENNY   185

Snag. That always got Percy excited. He thought Snag was *Mr. It*, all the time.

I ran down toward the creek with Percy in hot pursuit. He was huffing and puffing, and hollering for me to slow down. I did, but only long enough for him to catch up, telling him he had to run a little faster. I shouldn't have been in such a hurry. Little Percy was having a hard time keeping up.

In just a few minutes we came through the woods to the creek bank. Snag was already there with his favorite dog Skip, who was wet from chasing a stick into the creek and bringing it back. That dog loved the water about as much as we did!

Snag was laughing and shaking his head...looking me over as usual for any signs of a whupping.

"You know, Earl D., it's pure-dee amazing that we got out of that whole mess without even one little strapping from our pa's. Yep, pure-dee amazing! An' you know what else, old friend?"

I shook my head, no idea what he would say next.

"I'll have a humdinger of a story to tell my young'uns someday an' who knows, maybe even some grandkids if'n I don't get hung first!" He let out his usual crazy laugh and I joined him.

"Yeah, I know," I replied. "We're two lucky fellers. We coulda been in a heap of trouble there for a while. If you think about it, we could've crashed an' died. Then there would've been one of them sad funerals with Reverend Sparks praying for our departed souls an' the Sweeny's singing them mournful hymns."

"Yep," Sang spoke up. "Don't know if I'd want the Sweeny's to sing at my passing or not. You know how bad and sad they can sound at times, an' if'n it were me laying there in an ole pine box, they would do the worst they ever done when it comes to singing...juss to get even with me!"

186 JOSEPH A. JOHNSTON

I was laughing and Percy joined in, as I replied to Snag's last remarks, "Awww, Snag, you know good'n well that the Sweenys would be nice to you or anyone when it's something as serious as that. Let's talk about something else."

Snag took off on that notion. "Ya know, Earl D., we're luckier than a pair of hungry rats that fell into the corn crib, no doubt about it."

"Snag, I think I already said that, and I agree, but ole pal, what's for us to do tomorrow while we sit and wait for Chris and all the trucks and trailers to head out?" I asked.

"Mmmmm, tain't sure, but I think my pa has me hemmed up in a corner an' needin' some of my strong muscle power to fix the wagon bed. That doggone thing is about in splinters an' Ma told him she wasn't gonna ride in it another foot till he gets those old worn out planks and seat fixed. So, all I know is for you to drift over when ya can an' we'll ease down to the road an' maybe be able to wave bye-bye to 'em as they pass on up the road. Shore gonna be a lot of dust though, I betcha."

"Snag!" blurted Percy. "Tell me again 'bout how you and Earl D. got to fly in that aeroplane, please...okay?"

Snag began laughing as he led Percy over to an old felled log used for a firebreak when we occasionally had a small campfire for night fishing. There they sat down, Percy with his mouth hanging open, drooling, with his big eyes wide open. Snag began his tale. "Well, Percy my boy, it's like this. I, being a man of the world, felt it was about time to travel a different style rather than walking barefoot or riding a mule bareback. Now knowing what all I know about aeroplanes, it only seemed natchurl that I take charge of yore brother in this case, 'cause the boy don't know hoot 'bout

SNAG & ME – A FLYING IN A JENNY   187

aeroplanes...so, it's up to me to keep him safe and try to teach him a few things too—know what I mean?"

I was smiling big as ever, watching as my favorite pal Snag was doing it again to Percy. No telling what Percy was thinking from all these tall tales of Snag's, but for sure, they were big pictures in his mind.

After a bit, we headed back toward the house. Waving to Snag and Skip as they drifted off into the shadows of the late evening, we heading for home and the wonderful smells from the kitchen.

SUPPER TIME AROUND THE OLD TABLE

Mama's leftovers from dinner tasted good the second time around. Even the cornbread warmed up with a spread of butter tasted brand new to me.

Mama was telling us that she wanted to try and fix up another pie or two for Chris and his grandpa, if they would stop long enough to give it to them.

After cleaning up the dishes, Mama and Nell Faye lit into making two more pies. One blackberry and one peach. I had to do my part in this matter… go get some more stove wood. Boy, the kitchen was going to be blazing hot again. "Mama, after I get the wood in, I think I'll just sit on the back porch." She nodded her approval.

Sitting there with only a few shadows of daylight left, me and Percy were yakking about nothing important, but I was also thinking about when those fellers got those fresh pies of Mama's, they'd probably get into a fight as to who got a piece.

SEEING CHRIS BEFORE HE LEFT TOWN

We got to see Chris and his grandpa the next day as planned. Snag had ridden down to the park on his

188   JOSEPH A. JOHNSTON

mule, Lester, and had talked a bit with Chris about what time they would be leaving. Then Snag hi-tailed it over to our place to give us the news.

After church and dinner, Papa hitched up the wagon again and brought it around to the shady side of the house near the back steps. Mama gave me a large basket to set in the back with Percy and me. Then she and Nell Faye climbed on board. With a whistle from Papa, Charlie got the old wagon rolling down the lane. In just a bit we eased up close to the big road that goes to Bowieville, to wait.

As we sat there with just a slight breeze to lessen the heat, Snag and his folks joined us as well. It was hot as is it always is in July. Mama had her large parasol and we all tried to duck under it. 'Course, me, Papa and Little Percy had on our large straw hats, so that helped some. Snag had crawled under his wagon with some of his brothers as we all waited.

Then we got a surprise as we heard this racket. Lo and behold, here came the three little aeroplanes, all flying real low, one right behind the other, heading straight for us. We were jumping up and down waving as they flew right over our heads. There was that Capt. Ray B. waving and puffing on his cigar, then the little aeroplane with Miss Daring Dolly Dooley came zooming over us. This time she was sitting down in the front seat just a-waving. Mr. Warren LaBost was waving too. Finally the last little red aeroplane with Baron Von Thistle came zooming right over us and he was waving at us too. We just all stood there in the hot sun waving and carrying on until they were out of sight.

UP THE ROAD COMES A HERD OF TRUCKS

Snag and me were beside ourselves. That was some final show if ever there was one and all just for us. We

SNAG & ME – A FLYING IN A JENNY   189

turned as we heard Mama say something about a cloud of dust coming up the road. I knew it had to be Chris, his grandpa and all the other fellows in those big trucks. Sure enough, it was. In just a few minutes they came rumbling to a stop as Chris jumped out of a truck, running over to tell us all goodbye. He climbed up in the wagon to shake Papa's hand and hug Mama goodbye, and even gave Nell Faye a goodbye hug. He then did the same thing with the Galloway family. Now he was busy there to be sure with all the good byes. His grandpa was laughing, but telling him to get a move on too. At last we stood there sort of face-to-face for our last goodbye. He had tears in his eyes as we did too when he looked at us that final time to say goodbye.

"Earl D., Snag, I gotta tell you fellows something… I will never forget these past couple or three days because I have never had so much fun in such a short time or met a couple of fellows like you all. You both are top notch in my book. Now don't forget to write me a letter as soon as you can. I promise I'll do the same."

We shook his hand real hard and as before he gave us what he called a 'brotherly hug.' This caused us all to giggle a bit as he scurried back to their truck.

Mama got down from the wagon, gathered up the pies and came forth, giving them to Mr. Gus Sparks Einberger. "Sir, these are a couple of more pies I hope you and your folks will enjoy somewhere down the road."

Mr. Sparks thanked Mama and us several times as he was hollering and waving from the big truck.

Once again Chris climbed back up in the truck with his grandpa yelling all kinds of things for us to remember… mostly to stay good friends forever. Now that we'd surely do as we yelled out, "Chris… come back to see us sometime, and if you like, you can move up here from way down there in Florida!"

He was laughing, as the trucks started moving out again. They and all the trailers hooked up behind with the tankers and the trailer for the horses. And as they left, all the fellows were waving goodbye to us too. Big Jim was waving as he was trying to keep the old truck between the ruts in the road. We waved till our arms got tired.

It was a sad goodbye as all goodbyes are among dear friends. I knew we'd never forget the Little Trooper, as his grandpa called him. I was hoping we'd meet again. But if we didn't, then we'd meet him in heaven, for sure.

We sat there and chatted a bit until Papa said it was getting too hot to talk, so we waved goodbye to Snag and his family as they turned Lester around and headed back to their place. Papa turned Charlie around and headed our wagon for the cool shade in the backyard.

Yep, I had to admit, it was a great and fast adventure these past few days. So much to remember but for sure I would never forget them, especially that aeroplane ride and meeting a little fellow named Chris.

Growing up in Blanchard Forks was one big happy place to live. I was just so happy and thankful the Good Lord let me be who I was, having the best family and friends around, especially Snag. I only wished Chris didn't live so far away. If he lived close by, we could really have a bang up time every now and then. It would be super to have a pal like this who lived close by. Yep, growing up in Blanchard forks was about the best place in the world as far as I was concerned. To my way of thinking, God didn't make any better place in the whole wide world than right here! Yep, life was really good and I was real happy about being part of it.

~~~ The End ~~~

"Our Kind, Brave, Fun-loving Son." That's the epithet that sums up as best as we could in just a few words, the life of one of the most magnificent people we have ever known. We realize that we are his parents, but Christopher Patrick Becker truly was an outstanding 11 year old boy.

Chris was lucky enough to come into our lives just before we left active duty with the US Army. Before we settled down into what we thought would be a "normal" suburban lifestyle in Florida, we got a RV and roamed around North America for 7 months. As a 3 year old, Chris was able to visit all 50 states, each province in Canada, as well as each of the border-states in Mexico. Moving around with a toddler was a very rewarding experience, but, like most folks, we had to pick a place to live. We chose Tampa, where Chris enrolled in preschool, as we took up new careers.

Not too much later, Chris began to gradually become tired when playing, and his legs seemed to be always bruised. After an ear infection cleared as a result of medication, but his fatigue and bruising did not, we asked the pediatrician to do a routine blood test because we thought that perhaps he needed a vitamin or two. That led to an absolutely horrible day on what should have been his graduation from pre-kindergarten – the day that Chris was diagnosed with wide-spread neuroblastoma, a very aggressive childhood cancer – but a day that saved his life, at least for a while. He had multiple tumors in many different areas: bony areas, soft tissue, and even two thirds of the space where his bone marrow should have been had been replaced by the disease.

Over the course of the next nearly 6 years, Chris endured 34 cycles of chemotherapy – many of them were "high dose," in order to try to overtake the aggressiveness of this disease. He also underwent 3 major abdominal surgeries, which included the removal of his left kidney and adrenal gland, as well as ½ of his liver along with a brick-sized tumor. Chris endured two back-to-back stem cell transplants, using his own bone marrow stem cells to try to "jump start" his damaged immune and blood systems. He was subjected to two cycles of radiation therapy, as well as about 20 cycles of immunotherapy, which was offered only in New York. Then there were, of course, hundreds of blood and platelet transfusions, along with the bone marrow aspirates and various scans.

Yet, there was something about Chris that allowed him to do more than simply "endure" such hardships. After the first cycle of chemotherapy, Chris began feeling more like himself. He actually thrived during these difficult years.

Chris loved to move, dance, act and sing; he did so just about every opportunity that he had. Although the disease and/or its intensive treatments robbed him of the usual youthful stamina of most 5 – 11 year olds ("medium size kids," as he called them), Chris was able to lip-synch and break-dance to his favorite songs. He loved tae kwon do, which he started when he turned 5 years old because he liked the "cool moves" of the Power Rangers. Often bald and sometimes wearing a surgical mask during lessons, Chris steadily advanced through

SNAG & ME – A FLYING IN A JENNY   193

the ranks until he earned his First Degree Black Belt as a 9 year old. Chris also steadily worked his way through Cub Scouts, partly as a Lone Scout and partly as part of a regular pack, until he "crossed over" into becoming a Boy Scout a week before he passed away.

He had a wonderful gift of storytelling, which over the years evolved into stories such as "Me and My Big Fat Treehouse," "The Adventures of Superguy," and "Pixies: the Chamber of Stinkies." He also had a clever sense of humor, which complimented the stories as well as musical lyrics, which came so easily to him; Chris sometimes would just rattle off an entire song before the words could be captured in writing.

All of this came in handy as Chris made do with his very unusual lifestyle that revolved around treatment. The seriously suppressed immune system required that Chris' educational needs be met through a patchwork of Homebound Education, hospital teachers and any supplemental experiences that we provided whenever and wherever.

That didn't really bother Chris though, who looked forward to whatever new experiences each day brought. He had a smile or a joke for nearly every situation. In fact, he is still remembered locally and in New York as the boy who passed out smiley face pins to everyone he met. During his first hospitalization, medical technicians and nurses tried to alleviate his fears because they knew he'd have to spend a significant amount of time there. So they gave him trinket gifts at each scan or test to thank him for his cooperation. Even though he did not feel well, Chris wanted to give something back to people around him. It was his idea to have a bowl of chocolate "Hugs and Kisses from Chris" sitting in his room for the benefit of everyone who took care of him. It was also his idea to share a smile with everyone, especially those who looked like

194   JOSEPH A. JOHNSTON

they really needed one, so he began handing out smiley face pins to everyone. He truly gave them to everyone: other patients waiting in the same waiting room for their own tests or scans, and even tired waitresses at restaurants who looked like they could use a smile. That simple act by a child made most of those people return a real live smile back to him and perhaps with other people as well. Indeed, most of the medical people who took care of Chris at the two primary hospitals where he received care, still wear their smiley face pins on their lab coats or ID badges.

So what does all of this have to do with "Snag and Me?" Well, although they never got to meet in person, Chris came to the attention of Snag's and Earl D's creator, Grandpa Joe Johnston, by way of Chris' webpage, www.caringbridge.org/fl/chrisbecker. Once again, there was something about Chris' spunky spirit that caught his eye. Snag and Earl D., of course, belong to another era, one that seems to be genuinely nicer and friendlier than our current times. In their era, people still cared about what happened to their neighbors, and strangers were only folks that you hadn't met yet. Maybe the fact that Chris did the best he could with what he had, and truly never meant anyone any harm made "Grandpa Joe" think that Chris might like "Snag" and his fictional friends. You know, Chris did, too. He read each of the "Snag and Me" books prior to this one and seemed to like the slower times presented in those books.

Like Chris, Snag and Earl D. wanted to do good by doing well. Although these two guys bring smiles to the faces of those who read of their adventures, they can't really help anybody in a tangible way, at least not without your support. If they knew that there were other kids out there, who like Chris, spend many of their days locked up inside (whether in the hospital or at home) because their blood counts are too low for them to safely be able to play with other kids, they'd probably want to do something to help those kids. These are kids who should be playing tag, hanging a pole over a fishing hole, or even simply going to school, but instead are fighting for their lives. If they knew about it, maybe Snag and Earl D. would have scraped together a little bit, maybe even a little bit more if they told their families and neighbors to send some money to the National Childhood Cancer Foundation (www.curesearch.org) in order to help doctors try to stop neuroblastoma from killing other children like Chris. That would be of a lot of help, because less than 2% of all cancer research money (whether from federal or charitable origins) each year is spent on childhood cancer research, and that has to be further subdivided into each of the various childhood cancer specialties. That's true even though childhood cancer survivors could gain another 70+ years of life.

"Grandpa Joe" Johnston is going to help his buddies, Snag and Earl D., do just that. Simply by purchasing this book, you will be helping "Grandpa Joe" make a contribution to the National Childhood Cancer Foundation (www.curesearch.org) in memory of our kind, brave, fun-loving son. You can also do the same thing yourself, after purchasing and enjoying this edition of "Snag and Me," by contacting this organization directly. On its webpage, you'll find a link to "How You Can Help," which contains a number of different ways folks like you can help folks like Chris be able to live normal lives, kind of like Snag and Earl D.

Thanks for caring,

Alison and Pat Becker